Dropping Out

DROPPING OUT

Niamh Burns

Whiskey Tit
NYC & VT

Published in the United States and Canada by Whisk(e)y Tit: www.whiskeytit.com. If you wish to use or reproduce all or part of this book for any means, please let the author and publisher know. You're pretty much required to, legally.

ISBN 978-1-952600-23-4

Cover by Lissa McFarland.

For Deb

*Will there be no peace till I take this thing
out and kill it?*

*— The Downside of Being a Fuckup,
Wreckless Eric*

Chapter One

My father's death left me with a sense of urgency no amount of matured whisky could chide. Two weeks deceased and where had his life gone? A portrait hung in front of me at every meal, yet I'd never known him at all. The last time I saw him, I looked at the chiseled frame of his face as though for the first time. I closed my eyes tight against the memories.

The time he washed the vomit from my hair when my mom didn't want to touch me. She never wanted to reconcile the dirtiness that children left with them everywhere they went. It seemed he was always cleaning up her exasperation with the dirty dishes. He vouched for me — to get on baseball teams, to convince her I was worth spending a little extra money on so I could attend the extra-curricular classes I wanted to take. Allowing me the space to be the kind of man I wanted to be without forcing me to do anything to prove myself the way a lot of other men were expected to.

My dad taught me about women. He taught me how to respect them, and corrected my mistakes when I didn't. He loved my mom and sister exactly as they deserved. Ironic as it is, he was the only person that made me feel like part of the family. He kept my mom off my back when her distaste for me made its way past her fake, fake smile.

When I thought I screwed up everything he convinced her to let me back into the house. He picked me up from the ditches I threw myself into at my own volition. I could never have thanked him through the shame I felt.

He used to play music all the time, had an old beat-up guitar that he held onto with the same emotional attachment he had for me. The thing could've been replaced ten times over but it was always good enough for him. He filled the parts in me where my mom's love was supposed to rest. When I found out how much of his love for me was fabricated out of guilt I wanted to break everything that had once belonged to him, including myself. But even then, he picked up my pieces. I loved my dad more than anything that had ever entered my world even tentatively or from the imagination. I couldn't be awake without him. He never made me feel boxed-in or like a hand me down. He never measured my sister against me. We were just allowed to be.

Here now, awake without him, I'd surpassed the point of drunk where any and all is comprehensible, achieving that state of melodic drunk, a sloppy meditation of divided sleep and reality. I walked a few paces around my apartment, watching my solitary feet creak against the yellowing tiles. I was the only person who had visited me since I moved in. The floor was freckled with the stains of other people's lives, the only company I kept. I looked at the life-dyed pieces of linoleum and thought, maybe there are things to be feared more than failure. Maybe, when we're dead and moved on and out, the stains that only bleach could kill will fall down the well of the minds of those who survive us. With the moon a splinter in the sky, and my own flesh shriveling to the spine that held it, I felt only a narrow window connecting me to reality.

My mouth ached like one big abscess, and my eyes howled in compromise with their surrounding skin; bleak, terrible, dirty and isolated. My "home" had become one grand performance art piece in which I acted out how I felt inside, slowly over time. Cigarette butts I didn't remember stumping out littered the furniture handed down to me through some stranger at the thrift store. Newspapers slumped in the corner thumbed through and scribbled on when I couldn't keep my mind pickled in a jar. The mirror in the bathroom is what sold me on the place.

"We can have that replaced if you'd like." The landlord outlined the small crack running down the middle of the mirror. I smiled at my broken reflection: "When can I move in?"

Staring at my split reflection now I considered all the conflicting things I thought I knew about myself. I wanted the outcome of everything but never the process of getting there. Everything was an urgency, an instantaneous need. I knew what I wanted to be important to me, but not what was. Half of the mirror may as well have been blank.

I sat down on my floor and looked at my dad's old guitar case. I was too pissed off to open it before. My mom had dropped it off in the apartment lobby, with my dad's worst suit stuffed in a garbage bag next to it. She rang the buzzer and left before I had a chance to come out and meet her. She acted like my grieving had no place with hers, hadn't even called me when he died, left the hard stuff always up to my sister.

Now I opened the rusted latches, remembering the squeak of his hands moving along its neck and I felt him there for a minute. When I was a kid my dad would play restlessly, like an addict. My sister Angela grew bored quickly of the sound. She always was the practical one. I however stared in awe at my dad as he serenaded the room and grew twice the size of anybody I'd ever known. Giants exist where the soul is actualised.

Stuck inside the case there was a tiny note

folded and tucked between the strings. Had I known all along the reason he left me here ultimately? I fingered the edges, growing distant from my hands as I tried to escape the body holding it, simultaneously trying to reach closer through the abysmal space that connected life to death. The next thing I knew, I was pouring his words into my soul, desperate to find him again.

Rory,
Don't let where you came from stand in the way of all that you could be.
Dad.

For all the grief I carried I couldn't help but feel that his goodbye was cheap. My head in my hands, I wanted to carve my eyes out and take back what I'd read. I couldn't stomach the crawling sensation that comes with death. I read the note again and again hoping to find more, chasing each new rendition with booze and finding less coherent nothings. I rubbed my eyes hard and watched the stars fold themselves back into my brain.

Missing someone who's gone is the closest you can get to having them back again. The absence in your heart becomes so heavy, that bloody thing starts to feel like a large stone pendulum. Bruising your ribs and gashing your lungs with every swing-beat. There are poignant moments that invert you so far into yourself that you try to reach a part of you that never knew that person at all, just to stop the pain. I've heard rumors that you can reconcile this hurt, make peace with it, even find beauty in it. As my eyes traced the edges of my dad's final attempt to speak to me, I knew whoever said that was a fraud.

He couldn't have been less bothered. I tried to hold on to missing him but I couldn't help feeling exiled, the note meant little more to me than the sneeze that it was.

I hadn't given him much to hold on to. Over the past few years, I lost track of my heart. It's not easy to love someone, especially when you've got no other choice but to love them. Navigating that is intricate and fucked-up sometimes. My dad had a choice whether or not to love me. I never deserved how hard he tried. I stuck his pathetic 'see ya' to the wall next to my bed, ready to go mad over it.

Chapter Two

The last time I saw my dad was a completely irrelevant day on my calendar. I'd dreaded it because I always wanted to make him proud, but I was drinking again and I was failing university courses and still had no friends. I put on my best face and tried as much as I could to steady the pace of my drinking, enough to keep me from shaking and throwing aggravated stares at him, but not so much that he worried about me. I didn't need any more of that.

I loved seeing him because he was the one person who made me feel like I mattered, like the things I had to say might actually hold a bit of blubber. I never really let on that his acknowledgement of me was the main centre piece of my continued existence. I tried desperately to do things the right way. First year of university I got suspended for a semester for vomiting on my professor and telling him my emesis was more interesting than anything he had ever said. They let me back in on the premise that I would see an addictions counselor. I did that for about a month until they lost the extra time to care about me— I became a number to them again and I started back on the bottle. I kept this all from my dad, because as far as basic level functioning, I was just touching the bar and I was doing alright. Got out of bed most days, didn't get into as many fights and did my best to stay off the hard liquor, at least.

Small talk bubbled to the surface under all the unspoken anecdotes. He told me about live music he had checked out. For a long time, he lost interest in music, cared more about familial shit, parental backwash, being a good person. He rarely did anything for himself. He laughed in a curdled way, it sounded painful and bulimic. I watched, remembering snippets of time that held his fascination with sound, long since given up, tucked away, sat on, shit out, gone. His fingers still tapping in time to an invisible beat, his head bobbing every so often as though the spinal column were saxophonic.

The only constant was the faraway look in my dad's eyes. I couldn't figure out why he was saying anything he was saying, his sentences were illogical, missing large pieces, just floating words from his brain. The abyss between us caught what it could.

He told me about giving up love, about lost philosophy. I wish the verbatim was in me, as thick as the memory of sensation. I couldn't grasp him, was too focused on the inner wah-wah-wah monologue of Rory.

I had become busy. Too busy for my dad. Too busy to accept what love he had to offer me. Too guilty as well. After everything I had been through with him, the throwing of self at any hard surface that would mash me up a little, the running away. The betrayal of the trust and honour he placed on me that was never mine to begin with.

Due to my neverending preoccupation with the need to escape the real world, meetings between us had become rarities. I blamed it always on something I knew wasn't important. If you had told me then that my dad was going to die, I probably wouldn't have acted much different; I was too apathetic to do anything with that impending knowledge.

The thing about death: you can't warn anybody about it. Can't tell them it's coming. They'll hear you, sure, as clear as they can hear a creak in the wall, in the floorboard, and decide not to worry about it, go to sleep, turn up the movie. Then you can say, "Oh if I had known I would have hugged them harder, laughed louder at their jokes, maybe not let them out of my sight ever again." But would you? You probably wouldn't believe it. We don't believe in death until it's down our throats and in our eyes and everywhere, until it's ringing in our ears and dancing on our brains, threatening us with madness.

After an hour together, boy did he start talking fast and unimportantly. It was as though all the words coming out had been clotted in him. The definitive decision to end his relationship with existence left him unafraid to spew the crap about wanting to travel to Indonesia, about the girl he loved in college, the best friend he wished he called but who had long since died. The people I'd never heard of him knowing, who he regretted to stop knowing. The way he moved differently in the world as a man since he had me.

As always, I was too uncomfortable about my father acknowledging my existence to really let him get me, get through to me or make any noise beyond my dissociation. I kept him at a distance: mentally, physically, but emotionally not totally. I thought of him every day, even then. Not like now, where the thinking of him is louder than the whisky headaches, the swollen eyes and the wound renditions that keep being painted on my flesh. Bar fights, blackouts, forgetting. Anything that'll keep me away from really looking at the truth.

I can taste the last time I saw him more than I can picture it in my mind. The disgustingly sour and stale alfredo pasta, the cold garlic toast. The beer I shouldn't have drunk in front of him. He asked me something about if I was doing okay, if I was going to meetings. I told him something about having my drinking under control, as always. As though I ever had anything under control. He laughed at my jokes about college. He told me how he hated college, dropped out and became a dishwasher and then went back to pursue some bullshit accounting degree. Hated it more than the first time but saw it through so he could pay for his mom's chemo treatment. Told me how that was a waste because she died anyway. Then he cried and I played cheaply with the hem of my shirt. He talked to me about my mom because I didn't know how, didn't ever know how.

My dad didn't overdo his attempt at comforting me with positive affirmations. My sister Angela was the master of pep talks you didn't want. My dad, he never said anything he didn't believe for sure was true. And I think he knew as well as I did that my mom didn't love me the way she loved everybody else.

He tried to stuff as much of himself in those fragments of dialogue as he could. He told me a lot of stories that would never have come up naturally, like when he was in college, he had to write this essay on Christian dogma. He started to believe that people may all just be inherently quacked and trying really hard to get with something, anything, any set of rules that would send them on a guided tour of their own lives. People didn't like to be shuffled around mercilessly by unconfident folk, he said. They were much more akin to be chauffeured by people who at least could talk in a smooth enough circle to make you believe that if you wanted anything, it was to be guided by them. He went on and on about how taxing the research was, to wind up all for nothing.

A lot of his stories that day ended in things being all for nothing. I don't think my dad ever knew how much he had, or maybe I just didn't have a damn clue what he was missing. We can't measure another person's strength based on what we perceive them to have. When we envy the people we love, we wind up letting down those who need us most.

My dad stopped trusting men after I was born, I took up too much room in the house. He was so sensitive about my socialisation he stopped hanging around his work friends. I had next to no male influence aside from him and Jordan.

School came and went and every day he expected me to have socialised with someone, expected me to have some sort of record of all the interactions and connections I'd made with people that day. Unforeseen to me then, he was concerned about how their words and behaviours might filter through me and force me to be a different man than the one he was trying to mould me into. I had no idea then or now what kind of man that was. I was afraid of socialising the way my dad taught me to be, he acted so untrusting of every neighbour, check-out person and waiter that I didn't know how to trust either. I stopped trusting myself along the way as though my judgement wouldn't be good enough to bypass his screening.

He told me another story about the day I was born, and maybe on purpose, or maybe accidentally, how hesitant he and my mom had been about keeping me, how the decision wasn't so ultimately theirs as it had seemed to be made by fate. My mom was on the defence and insisted on seeing me through, how the roles instantly switched when I was born. He put me in my mom's arms and he swore he saw some sort of spatial shift in the room, like it doubled in size and then shrunk down to fit her frame completely, "hugged the both of you in some cosmic acceptance" my dad said, over his cold plate of untouched food. He told me how when he saw us together, he wanted to stop the Earth and let us all get off so we could stay like that forever without ever having to face what may or may not develop outside of the room, once the pain killers had worn off.

He told me how much he loved my mom and he cried again. I tried to reach him through whatever strange substance sat between us but I couldn't. I loved my mom in this painful and corrosive way, where she burned me at my every attempt to breathe her air and I wanted nothing more than just to know any one simple thing about her. I learned that day, as my dad said, she loved with a force that closed her off completely. Something that paralysed her and kept her from naturally expressing it. She did it in a different way, by the things she'd do for you. She never was a hugger or a coddler, no pretty words and phrases and birthday cards. I think he said all this to make me feel better, because observation proved to me I was the only one she loved in this cold, hard way. I believe he believed that she did love me different, and that if he could talk enough in one of those melodic circles, I would accept that as being enough.

Retrospectively, almost every story, every bit of rambling, ranty, sometimes off-putting and annoying bit of dialogue we shared that day, was a goodbye. A warning that I wouldn't have his advice, unwanted or not, ever again. The last thing I remember my dad saying to me was that I looked exactly like my mom, and that relieved him year by year as he watched me grow up. He told me I was handsome and to take care of myself. He told me that the thing my mom did to express her love was keeping me for all these years, as though this guilt trip was supposed to make her continuing to look at me periodically feel like some sort of gratifying gift to my spirit.

Chapter Three

Stinking and exhausted, dragging the body from bed to class to ceaseless misery. My eyelids beat down on my vision that morning, one grand vessel tightened by alcohol and tears, pulsing through my loud, tired head. According to the calendar I was on day three of not handing in my paper on Plato's forms. So far, I had lost fifteen percent of the hypothetical grade I didn't care about.

"Hey Dr. Smolinsky." A stitch rose up in my side as I tried to catch up with him. "I was wondering if I could get another extension?"

"Of course, kid, of course. It's fine, it's fine. Get it to me by tomorrow's end." He didn't look up when he spoke to me, addressing instead a stack of papers in his hand. "Thanks Gary, I'll see you next class." He patted me on the shoulder and walked away. No care for the deadline long drowning me, the paper in question or my identity in the midst.

Smolinsky was my favourite professor because every time I met him I got to be a new person. He didn't answer emails, remember anyone's name or make any appearance that he knew where he was at all. I love people who work jobs they should have been retired from for years. One morning I showed up twenty minutes late to class and Smolinsky glared at me for about thirty seconds and then asked me if I was lost. That day I became Troy. I kept a small list in my head of all my personas. Troy, Ron, Robert, Ronan, Gary.

I made my way to the library, took the stairs all the way up to the fifth floor to work off some drunkenness, leave enough to survive my own mind. Thinking with each step that it was useless to even try to write a paper on something I couldn't begin to understand. Maybe instead I would spend hours finding nirvana amongst the shelves of great epics. Pouring over volumes of William Blake, reflecting on the nature of the mind.

The first Blake I ever read was *Auguries of Innocence*. 'To see a World in a Grain of sand / And a Heaven in a Wild Flower / Hold Infinity in the palm of your hand / And Eternity in an hour.' At the time I was seventeen years old and the one hundred and twenty-eight lines that follow these ones were lost on me. That was the moment poetry became something real in my life. In between the lines of verse, I could feel that Blake knew more about reality than I ever had. It comforted me to know that lost as I was in my conscious brain, a deeper layer of myself was nodding in agreement with him, and whatever part of me that was, wasn't so lost.

Now that time had surfed past that version of me, whenever I read Blake, I felt the split in the centre of the universe, where one side had tribulation and sacrifice making a mess of man, the other was privy to easy and honest contentment, and I always found myself longing to swim somewhere in the middle.

"Hey? Hello?"

My skin scalded my bones as I fell back into my body clumsily, looking up at a creature sewn from silk. "He-" I cleared my throat. "Hi, yeah, hey." I held out my hand and quickly withdrew it, dabbing whisky I wasn't aware of drinking from my lips.

"Oh- sorry, you just dropped your notebook." Her eyes fluttered over the surface of mine so briefly that I finally understood what it felt like to want to hold the finite for an infinity.

I grabbed it more aggressively than I meant to, almost flinging it back out of my hand. Her eyebrows joined each other in judgement of me. "Alright then, see you."

I resented spending so much time in the other worlds I flitted in and out of instead of preparing to be in the one people like her existed in. I rubbed my jaw, sore from tensing against the embarrassing choreography of my tongue. I dragged my hungover bruise of a body to a table and prepared to sneeze out a paper. My eyes blurred every word on the screen whenever I pulled up the rubric. My mind held me hostage with thoughts of the girl I just met, and I found myself touching the spots on my notebook where her fingerprints had traveled. I dragged my sore, stiff arm across the page trying to disengage myself with the frustration of my own mind.

"Oh my god he texted me back!" Two girls sat behind me, waking the worms that occupied the rat hole rage portion of skull.

"Read it out loud!" Squeal.

I watched the heartbeat of that thin line on a word document, the stagnation of writing. Tick, tick, tick.

"Ask him to come to the library, do it, do it, do it."

Trying to keep my composure, I looked around for a minute. There was a guy completely engaged with his cell phone in the corner and I felt irrationally furious with him. I loathed the frequency at which philosophy brainwashed me. As soon as I did 3.25 minutes of reading my brain went 'Ah, we are much more intelligent than the rest of these half breathing fish' and I started to think like a damned fool. Philosophy was not supposed to be so ego-charged. The sound of everyone's breathing radiated through my skull. I took a deep breath, remembering the many places my anger had taken me in the past that I just couldn't afford to go anymore.

I shut my mind to the giggles, the chirping, clicking, muttering of the people around me and begged my motivation not to hang itself.

"Give me your phone."

"No you're gonna mess my relationship up."

Mind balled into a fist. Whisky carved a hole through me where I could lay down and rest awhile. I took a swig from my coffee mug to calm the pulse of my brain in its big tube. I could only tell I was getting drunk by the way my hair caked with sweat to my forehead, body always a temperature higher than it should be, but never feeling as under the weather as I wished. I wanted so badly to disappear. The burning in my throat kept everyone out for fragments of time, so I took longer gulps.

The ringing in my ears started to dissipate, and the sounds of the room got louder as the throbbing of my head went to rest. I walked over to where the two girls were sitting. One looked a lot braver than the other, like she bullied people to be friends with her and on a good day they chose to, out of respect rather than fear. Her nostrils were permanently dilated with the unavoidable stench of pretension that followed her around. The other girl looked uncomfortable sitting there in the suit of her own skin and was hesitant to rest her eyes on anything for longer than half a second.

"Hey, I'm just trying to finish a paper here, could you keep it down?" I could feel the spirit of my voice separating itself from me, wobbling with the whisky.

One of the girls looked up at me innocently while the other started to giggle. I rolled my eyes and went back to my work wishing desperately that I had headphones. Or earplugs. Or a gun to shoot myself with.

"Oh my god, that guy was so hot." One of them giggled.

"He's not even that hot."

"Yeah he is actually pretty hot."

"Maybe if you get hit in the head."

I took a deep breath, ready to yell out loud. Too embarrassed now to turn around I got back to ripping my hair out at this paper. My fucking ideal is for everyone to shut their mouths until they've truly come up with something worthwhile to say. Even then they can save it for someone else. My ideal is to not exist at all.

"Horizontal stretch-"

"Yeah, it's being stretched by two."

"How is this hard to understand? It's pretty obvious."

They were almost yelling this time, I couldn't

believe how easy it was for them to bounce so quickly from one irritating bit to the next.

"You know this is a library right?"

"Yes, pretty boy. Thanks for the update. You're a prick. Stop talking to me."

I could feel my voice trembling in my throat, overwhelmed by everything in my external vicinity. "Please just keep it down. Some of us actually want to work."

If there was anything about school that I hated more than the demands and the pressure and the course work, it was the people who occupied the space. My dad told me once that your ability to succeed lay mostly in how capable you were of tolerating those that surround you on your journey. You can't always pick your associates. Well, fuck him. I wasn't capable of tolerance or success. I worked hard to fit in yet another place I wasn't built to belong. Another long kiss, allowing the hot liquid to remove my guilt or any potential utterances of profanity from my tongue was all I was capable of then. Moment by moment, the girls built up steam, intentionally creeping under my skin. The melody in my head started to screech like nails against pavement. It was happening again, creeping through my throat and dragging me out of my body.

"Can you shut the fuck up?" My lips were dancing with a voice like mine, coming through the mesh of my ear somewhere far beyond. Hands slamming on the table, whisky at my feet soaking calves and untidy dress shoes.

The guy diagonal from me looked up from his phone, brow still furrowed, looking annoyed at reality. Both girls looked at me wide eyed and then at each other, laughing, mocking me three times at once in the dizziness of the hall.

"Just shut up, just shut the fuck up. Fuck you." Control was lost, brakes were broken, I started to cry disgusting phlegmy tears straight from the gutter of my grief.

"Wow that guy is fucking out of control. What a crazy douchebag."

"Yeah but he's pretty though."

"Doesn't matter how pretty you are if you're an ugly fuck on the inside."

Who was talking anymore? And who could care? I picked up my coffee mug and sucked what was left from, inhaling liquor, floor hair on my lips, coating tongue with offered help. "You have no idea what you're talking about just shut the fuck up." I held the table and felt it shake, threatening to come loose from the metal plates that held it into the ground.

"Dude take a chill pill. You're fucking psychotic." Smiles ran off their faces in twos, my mouth, loose at the edges, allowing the pit of me to come out loud as my eyes rolled in my face losing control under the flood.

"What is wrong with you? Are you crying?" She laughed in a scared way.

"You need to fuck off. Just shut the fuck up. Just fuck off." My feet were yelling, mouth falling to the floor, the table watched and mocked as I screamed incomprehensibly through my phlegm hands.

"Excuse me sir, you're going to have to leave." A heavyset man blanketed me with his shadow, his voice skipping away from itself, my ears too loud. Brain is bleeding.

"Sir have you been drinking?"

I rolled my tongue around the shavings of my mouth, spitting skin onto my lips, him swimming in my eyes. Abstract lungs sealed shut in my chest emitting tears from the lesions in my face. Dad would say I've come too far and the man has come to take my balls.

"Hello, sir?"

"No." One of my eyes met his, he was standing on either side of himself. "No I haven't been drinking."

He sniffed my coffee mug. "No?"

"Awww man where did you get that? 'Smine."

"Do you go here?"

"I don't fucking think so." Laughter belched through the crack in my face, dripped down the snot on my cheeks.

"Do you have ID on you?"

I threw my student ID at him. "So you do go here? I'm going to have to ask you to leave."

"I can't go now, I have a paper due. I gotta do it man, for 'them'"

"Uh-huh. Well you'll have to do it somewhere else." He tried to pull me up by the arm.

"I can't go. They have to go." I pointed at the girls, glued to their seats now, watching every minute detail to later reiterate in their gossip circle.

"Alright, let's go buddy. You're very drunk. You're violating school property. Time to go."

I pushed him away and stood up to face him. "I don't care."

"Fascinating. Let's go." My insignificance was boiling hot, I gave him my arm, limping lifeless next to it — dragging self from lobby to lobby, shimmering faces repeating and blending with the sweat in my eyes. My face was snot, and heaven reached me again as I dripped down all five flights of humiliation. The girl who touched my notebook. I tried so hard to pretend her eyes were full of sympathy instead of absolute disgust and vicarious embarrassment. After all, there must be an ideal, unchanging perfect form of this situation that can be retrospectively actualised.

Chapter Four

"Hey dad I'm gonna go out with some friends tonight, is that okay?"

"Which friends?" He looked up from the papers littering his desk.

"Just Jordan." He accepted this, even though I was a shit liar. I knew Jordan wouldn't be there. He made a really firm point that he would never be dragged to another dumb high school party.

"I don't want to be your babysitter," he had said to me. As though I acted out, profane and insane. I was just having fun and any sucker could see that. Sometimes I thought Jordan might not be the friend for me. The other guys really seemed to think I was a riot, they appreciated me, even when I was coming undone. Plus Jordan had never even seen me drunk, he was only judging me off the shit he heard from other people.

"Be home by midnight."

I was out the door racing down the lawn, excited like you get when you're a kid hoping that they give out bribes at your classmate's birthday party so that it would be worth your time going, little bags with candy and stickers, something to be earned for being social.

"Fuck YES. Rory's here. Now the real party has started." Ian slapped me on the back, shoving a solo cup in my hand as I walked through the door.

"What's this?"

"Ha. Yeah like you care, drink up my dude."

I complied, even though I was still a little uneasy about getting drunk. I didn't like that beginning dizzy feeling, like someone had hit you over the head or like your brain was sitting in a bucket of dirty water. I drank it slowly and nervously, my eyes watering a bit. No one was paying attention but I saw how they treated Jamie when he tried to stay true to his limits. He was exiled from the gang, I didn't want that, I'd worked so hard to get here.

When I was a little kid, I had no friends. People thought I was a loser. Just that little kid at the back who reads and thinks and zones out all the time. I was confused every day because I couldn't focus long enough on any one thing to catch up to reality. This was an easy trait to mock. Even for most of high school I was a loner, sitting at the back, trying to ignore as many people as possible except Jordan, who I couldn't even bring up around these guys.

Jordan came from a rough life; his parents were both alcoholics and had to give him up. He was sent to foster care when he was eight, which we both reached the conclusion we were grateful for because otherwise we wouldn't have met. He said I was the brother for his soul. But the system ended up giving him to more alcoholics. Really reliable, functional alcoholics, the kind that can pass a house inspection and lie really well to anyone in charge of anything. The kind of people who have jobs and nice cars and a nice house. The kind that says they aren't alcoholics because they only drink in the evening. The kind that put really expensive nice paintings over the holes in the plaster.

Because of his upbringing and the people around him, Jordan never wanted to drink. He didn't have an interest in even trying a drop. "Alcohol tore my life apart, Rory. I watched what it did to my parents when I was a little kid. They lost me and I lost them because of this shit. Now I'm stuck with these strangers who aren't even honest about how deranged they are and that's way worse if you ask me. Alcohol turns people into strangers, it makes it impossible to know yourself."

People made fun of Jordan because he didn't drink. He didn't smoke weed, he just listened to jazz. He had too many opinions and wasn't afraid to express them. He was smart, had an encyclopaedic knowledge that comes with having no one to talk to growing up. He wanted to know everyone's life story and he asked the strangest questions, wanting to know the deepest things about a person. That's the way that Jordan got drunk.

I wanted somewhere bigger to escape to, somewhere I was accepted by a group of people who seemed to know a thing or two about acceptance. It started by accident, really. I never wanted to drink, just wanted to keep my head down everywhere I went and try to get through life making as little a disturbance as possible.

People didn't like me and I knew that. I faltered when I spoke, never sure of what I wanted to say. That changed when I was invited to a party at Ian's, that popular, self-righteous jock everyone knows in one form or other. I knew that it was a joke, my being invited, but I wanted to go anyways to prove to them and myself that I wasn't the loser they all thought I was. Jordan tried to talk me out of going.

"Why do you even care what those idiots think? They're all at the peak of their life right now. It's pathetic. You have potential to get past this high school shit. Rational people are able to see that high school is just a dumb awkward few years of their lives that come before them really finding themselves. Those dick bags think that this is the most important part of their lives. They don't know what they're talking about anyway. You're cool shit man, you don't need them."

I responded by trying to convince him to come

along with me. I tried to mask my true want to be accepted by them by saying that it would be funny if we went, we could show them up by acting like huge freaks, we could make fun of them.

"That's a waste of time man, I'm not interested. Seriously though, if you're gonna go be careful. Those assholes don't give a shit about you, you gotta remember that."

So I went to the party, against my own advice and Jordan's. Against any inner voice that told me it didn't matter what a bunch of shallow idiots thought of me, it only mattered insofar as I was tired of being bullied, when I never got a break from it. I went home and got bullied by my own mind, my mother ignored me, I was bullied by my own expectations of fitting in, manipulated and coerced myself constantly to pretend that everything was okay no matter how not okay it was. School was the least peaceful place for me, and I was willing to do pretty much anything to make it more peaceful so I could have some place in life that felt like my own.

The first hour or so of being at the party was so uncomfortable I felt like any single thing I ever hated about myself was highlighted for the world to see. I could feel myself getting uglier and uglier every time someone looked at me. I tried to smile at people but it came out as a cringe and no one would talk to me.

The house was fancy enough, as you'd expect

from a kid who was well-liked for no obvious reason. I mean, Ian was never nice to anyone, not even his closest friends. Everything he said came out as a jeer, or a provocation. People worshipped him like some sort of demigod just because he was rich and coercive. His parents had a pool, let him throw parties, neglected him enough to make him mean and likeable because he was always able to bribe people with the facilities of his life. All the same, I wanted his acceptance as much as the next idiot.

People were having fun all around me. I tried to spot another person who looked as out of place as I felt, and couldn't. Everyone knew someone, liked someone, had someone to talk to. I had the wall and the weird creepy hand-carved shelf that stood next to me obscuring part of the room from my sight. I was surrounded by people I could never relate to, desperate to find one thing I could use to bridge that gap.

I thought about leaving but then I thought too much about leaving and realised how weird it would look if I left. All I had done for an hour was stand in the corner worrying about my feet being too big, and I couldn't help but think that everyone knew exactly what had been going through my head. I was embarrassed to be around these people. I felt like my head was a giant pimple.

I had to try to act natural. I focused on how many bathroom breaks I took. When I got nervous I peed a lot, but I didn't want anyone to know that. I tried to tell myself that no one was paying attention to me but I could feel all the eyes in the room on my face even when no one was looking at me at all.

I walked over to the table with the drinks, tried to act like I did this all the time. Poured half the glass full with rum, the other half with coke, choked on the taste. It tasted the way I'd expect lighter fluid to taste. I was gagging. A dude next to me was laughing.

"Wow you got way ahead of yourself there bud."

"Nah, I always drink this much."

"Oh yeah?" he smirked at me. "Here's a beer to chase it with."

"Okay thanks." I opened the beer and took a sip. It tasted like fermented cow food and poison. I held it in my mouth hoping the taste would settle down, hoping I could swallow it without puking it straight back up. The guy was watching me the whole time. I didn't want to look straight at him in case he saw how much my eyes were watering. I took another small sip from my solo cup, another sip from the beer. He invited me to come hang out in the backyard with the guys.

Ian's backyard was bigger than my entire childhood home. He had a pool, a guest house, a huge firepit. We walked over to the fire, and sat down next to a group of people that to my relief all ignored my arrival. The whole time they were talking about sports and girls and things I knew nothing about. I was too nervous to say anything and I didn't know what I was supposed to be doing with my hands so I just kept sipping the drink that tasted so horrible. My heart started beating weirdly and slowly and the whole party seemed to feel a lot better.

At some point I had four solo cups stacked on top of each other and I was talking fast and excitedly, telling some story about something I had never actually done. People were listening to me, they were laughing with me, they were encouraging me to drink more. We started doing shots. I started losing the words I was saying as quick as they were coming out of my lips.

"Man, Rory, you're a fucking good time." Ian said to me, grabbing me tight around my undeveloped bicep. "I was totally wrong about you; you're welcome around here any time."

At some point in the night people were holding the bottom of a ladder while I climbed to the top, screamed "fuck it" as loud as I could and was soaring off the roof of Ian's guest house with my arms spread wide, landing on the fake rich people grass. People were laughing, hooting, checking on me to make sure I was okay, calling me a hero.

Everyone at school heard about my presence at this party, people who weren't there were yearning to be able to go back in time to witness it all. The only person who wasn't impressed with me was Jordan. He wasn't really mad at me, just changed the subject when it was brought up, and rolled his eyes when I tried to tell him it was no big deal, tried to tell him that I hated the attention I was getting.

Ian wanted me to hang with him and the guys every weekend. Though I wasn't sure I liked the feeling alcohol gave me, it was just a gateway to having a social circle to call my own. Drinking wasn't a big deal anyways, everyone did it all the time, it was just something you did at that age and if it could bridge the gap between my awkwardness and my heroicness then it was really the best thing to ever happen to me.

I became the most popular person at these parties somehow. I was invited all the time and people rejoiced at my arrival. I kept trying to tell Jordan that I hated the attention, wanted no part of it, but he didn't buy it any more than I did.

I lost large chunks of memory of my high school years to these parties but it was all worth it when I came to school and was greeted kindly, almost worshipped by some people. I had climbed the social ladder so quickly I was almost as high up as Ian. It was the first time in my entire life I ever felt like people found me worth knowing or spending time with. I didn't feel so weird all the time. My confidence grew, I could carry myself through the world on my own shoulders without flinching. I never wanted to go back to when I had no clue what this felt like.

Nothing could last, like nothing ever did.

Eventually I couldn't spell my own name in the mud when I got drunk. I didn't know how to stop drinking because I thought the more I got down the hatch, the more people would like me. There was a line I apparently couldn't see. I became the angry guy, the weird guy, the guy who talked in circles. Alcohol did something to me that it didn't seem to do to anyone else around me. It made me lose parts of my cognition, it made me do things I wasn't comfortable doing, it made me remember things that weren't my own memories. It made me see things that weren't really there.

Jordan stuck by my side through it all, even when I was being the type of irritating person that he hated the most. All the other people I hung out with started dropping off quickly, going back to mocking me but now with an inner knowledge to mock me from. Things were getting worse. Jordan tried to tell me that I had tried something, that it didn't work out and that's just the way that life is sometimes, but I couldn't help it, thinking that if I kept drinking, I could find that place again where everything felt so good.

Chapter Five

"Nothing is linear or real anymore." Whisky glasses hold excellent conversations, opportunities for deepest intimacy and connection. Pure unadulterated honesty. The unveiling of what our primal selves want. Desire can't unmask healthily anymore because of the facets of information being poured on us, the unending unrelenting to-do lists and must-haves and must-bes of our fake, fake lives.

"Maybe it's time I cut you off?"

"I'm fine. I'll have another." I wasn't brave enough to meet her eye. I learned the hard way that love wasn't my forte. I liked my art on a faraway wall, not so that I couldn't hold myself accountable in admiring it, but so that I could admire it without asking it to peel itself from the plaster which held it high. In doing that, I never had to worry about dropping it, scratching the paint, or damaging it irreversibly in some other clumsy way.

I don't remember how I got where I was. Bleary

eyes meet bleary eyes. Thursday nights are for getting drunk. So are Wednesdays, Tuesdays, Mondays and Saturdays. Mornings are alright too.

"Wasyer name?"

"Claire." She spoke not to me, but at me out of obligation, the end of her speech dropping with a definiteness that wanted me gone. "Can I call you a cab? We're closing up now and that guy left hours ago."

I stared at the door tracing it for the memory of the hours leading up to where I was then. I felt footsteps on the floor below me, from long ago and far off. I looked down at my hands, clammy and dead with cold. My blood was all in my brain, making my eyes go crazy in the whirlpool of my head. I swam back to look at Claire, polishing a tumbler with her dainty hands, the squeaking of the glass and the clink as one met another.

"What guy?" I could sense him vaguely, a silhouette of a person, the way you'd remember someone you only dreamt of.

"Chuck. His name's Chuck. You know, tall biker dude. He's in here all the time." She threw a cloth over her shoulder as I rolled the name over my tongue, Chuck, Chuck, Chuck.

Tonight was an appropriate night for a homesickness of the flesh. I had walked straight from my apartment, wearing my father's suit. I only put it on when I missed him most, which incidentally left me wearing the wrinkled thing for the past four days. The opening hymn-like synth of Blue Monday was coming through the windows of a bar called Tavern. The song came out raunchier and without much rhythm, cutting in and out of old speakers. I started missing people I had no business missing, like my ex-girlfriend and the urgency she used to kiss me with. The fleeting months and years of passionate love that roll by you and cough dust in your face. The could-have-been moments of my earlier youth: cheeks pressed against cheeks and warm bodies cradling one another in orgasm and ecstasy.

"Move, stupid prick." A girl with short blue hair pushed past me as I stood in the middle of the bar, a lost child seeing the world for the first time. All around me were booths with peeling leather seats, blood red walls, crooked framed posters, chipped wood tables, sticky floors and the whole place reeking with pre-regret. It was small, cluttered and perfect.

Slumped at the bar was a man with thick black hair held still atop a spine made of piano keys. He moved pentatonic with the rhythm of his drinking. One hand up, head slunk down, curling with the sway and pull of alcohol. The arches of his shoulders seemed to age as I sat there, hunching lower and lower as my experience of him heightened in his expiration. He wore a jacket, leather and ratted like the barstool beneath him. Well-worn and weather broken, his skin must have been twelve layers thick, rubbed raw with life.

"Can I get a shot of Jack?" The bartender placed it in front of me without acknowledgment. I had always found the act of writing in bars pretentious, show off-y and irritating. Nevertheless I scratched pencil against pad trying to organise a coherence that was hand-in-able.

"You should be more direct. None of this semi-colon shit. Get to your point." The man next to me was drumming his fingers on the table, leaning over to read my work. He looked at me out of the corner of his eye, laughing without making a sound. When he grinned, he showed off a gallery of worn teeth, concealed behind cracking dry lips, dim lanterns hid in the recessions of his face, old compasses hiding in the pockets of his skin. I drank without looking straight at him, gazing at him through the fog of the glass.

"So what's the deal with all this? Theory of Forms, what a load of horse shit." He motioned at me with the hand that held his drink, sopping the contents all over his arm and licking it off his coat sleeve.

I picked up a peanut from the bowl in front of me, more for something to do with my hands and somewhere to rest my eyes than because of any appetite compulsion.

"It's for school." I put the peanut in my mouth and spat the stale thing back into my hand, all at once aware of how my dad's suit hung off me like an overworn bathrobe.

"Ah, school." He laughed.

"I just came for a drink, lay off me would ya?"

He picked up my notebook and started flipping through it, my body buzzed with apprehension. "Geeze kid, what's eaten a hole in your ass? *This magic at once in the morning constitutes as another field for regret to chase us down, awakeness and solitude ending at once, once we feel the full weight of death on us.* Someone's having a dark night of the soul."

I grabbed my book back from him, slammed it shut and drank slowly, glaring at the wall hoping if I stared long enough, he would disappear.

"My dad killed himself." We both fell silent.

"I'm sorry, that's rough." I could feel him trying to stare through me. I was annoyed and his gaze made me feel sticky.

"Yeah, well life goes on right? Besides, we all act like we're already dead. So maybe death doesn't make much difference."

"The hell's that mean? If you're acting like you're already dead, you've got some soul searching to do."

I glared at him head on now. "Think about it. We gotta get up in the morning, we gotta go to school or work or whatever other building wants to churn us into meat for society. We have to be brilliant and we have to be bold but not too bold or someone will catch on that we're different."

"I've never done any of that shit, and I'm just fine. It's ego-material shit kid, wipe it off your ass."

"Well I have to do that shit."

"You know this Theory of Forms you write about, it's not meant to be taught in a school. A little bit ironic if you ask me."

"What do you mean?"

"I mean, the whole theory revolves around this realm of forms where our souls lived before they experienced amnesia after being vacuumed into these skin vials, our lives are spent recalling the forms. Plato himself said they can't be educated. So if your soul isn't in the place to recall the forms, you just fuckin' won't."

"I guess that'd be relevant if you believe the theory."

"Why would you be studying something you don't believe?"

"I don't know what I believe. It's part of the curriculum. What the fuck do you know anyway?"

"I know as much as you, as much as anyone."

I went back to my writing, more self-conscious than I had been when I walked in.

"Kid, listen," he went on. "I studied philosophy in school, then I realised fuck this why am I paying thousands of dollars to learn shit I could learn better at a library?"

"It's not like they give you space in school to

learn it anyways, you just have to regurgitate what they want to hear."

"See? You already know." He lifted his glass to clink against mine. "My name's Chuck."

"Rory."

"Rory, you've got a long road ahead of you if you think you're not too smart for school."

"I've got an even longer road ahead of me if I think I'm too smart for it."

"We all are. What, do you think we can worship these teachers like they're some sort of God? That's egotism. Narcissism at best. If you ask me it's all horseshit."

"Well I didn't ask you."

He grinned. "Nah, you didn't, did you?"

"It's not like I like school. That's not why I'm there."

"Then why are you there?"

"For my dad."

"Your dad's dead."

"Yeah, thanks asshole. It would have made him happy."

"You know, if you were happy and doing some shit that fulfilled you, I bet that would have made him a hell of a lot happier."

I found myself wanting to pour my heart out to Chuck. He had a cool way of carrying himself, like hell could pass right through him and he wouldn't feel it. "I just have to do something. My mom fucking hates me, my sister's a great success and I just sit around destroying myself."

"You think school's gonna stop you destroying yourself?"

"Something's got to."

"You're looking in the wrong place, dude."

"It keeps me from being alone."

"Nothing can keep someone from being alone. Nothing."

The memory was hazy, the night was hazy. I was swimming through different versions of myself all stuck in a pile. I remember reaching some conclusion and then losing it. I remember thinking over and over again, nothing can keep someone from being alone. Nothing. I shivered, and disbelieved it for lack of a better understanding. Thinking about my aloneness made the world swell under my feet. I couldn't tolerate it. I had to think even if the shit I was doing was useless it was better than doing nothing, better than just letting myself rot as the centrepiece of my life.

"Seriously, you have to leave. We're closing."

I self-consciously snapped my mouth shut, realizing the disembodied voice flying between my lips had been sharing intimacy I didn't know I had.

"Claire." Her name fell easily off my swollen, dry tongue. "Can you call me that cab?"

"I know you're not asking my advice but you should try to keep some of that shit for yourself."

"Some of what shit?"

"Anything. Just keep some things to yourself." She looked at me long and tired, drilling self-consciousness through my pupils but I couldn't feel it any more than I could remember what I'd done to be embarrassed about.

"Just don't piss where you sleep or whatever." She pointed at the cab outside and nodded for me to go meet it.

Chapter Six

The real world is of ideas, not senses. If Plato's theory of forms isn't completely useless then this paper is already in existence somewhere in time and space and needs only to be re-written in the physical. And if his theory of forms isn't useless then I'll inevitably drop out of school anyways because somewhere I know that fabrication is subjectively terrible and a plot to render our truth meaningless– in simpler terms: institution is made up. But I can't say I understand the forms anyway.

Angela's calling again. She's been doing that for days now. I guess the guilt finally struck even with her anger and now she's trying to save my life again. I pace my apartment; I feel my ankles crack and I give in to the urge to scratch my skin raw. There's blood under my nails and little droplets fall onto my phone screen as it lights up and I press the red button to ignore her. I wasn't in the mood to talk about what my sister thought she may or may not know about what's best for me.

My head was pounding under a clenched fist and I wanted to get this stupid paper out of me so I could move on with my life. But I just kept beginning it and then throwing it away. What did Plato mean by Forms? My phone started ringing again. I started to write. Plato theorised that the soul existed in a space where all knowledge was eternal. My heart was pulsing, I kept standing up, being suffocated by my surroundings and then sitting back down again, the blood pooling between my ears and behind my eyes. All I wanted to do was succeed at something, or maybe drown my mind in as many ways possible so I didn't have to think anymore. Any time the real world dragged me back into it, I couldn't stop thinking about my father and thinking about him occurred in my chest. I walked through my apartment, bending my sore legs slowly, stretching my exhausted hips. I ripped his hideous goodbye off my wall and tore it into pieces, threw it in the toilet, pissed on it and flushed it. Fucking asshole left me with nothing but guilt, indecision and an all-encompassing loathing for the world.

I dumped the last of my vodka on the essay, surrendered to never writing it as I walked over to the mantel to get my keys. A destination in mind now, thick on my tongue. My old friend Jordan would say, "If someone cares about you, they'll show it all the time, not just when they're feeling guilty." I picked up the picture I had of Jordan and I on my mantel. I used the sharp edge of the wooden frame to chip away at the skin on my fingers. We had been friends all our lives. At a time, we were inseparable but that was before I became prone to throwing fits every day. He made me feel like I belonged somewhere. I hadn't called him since the incident.

Jordan saved me from a crisis that was only comparable to the one I was having now. Kicked out of one set of doors, into another, rushed from ambulance to hospital. Skin stitched, stomach pumped. Once released, more alcohol to soothe the ache. I tried in vain to exist in the world but never could look at my reflection without feeling guilty for other people's wrongs. I tried to push my soul back out of the tube of my body but it stayed there, stagnated only to sleep and woke me up with Jordan next to my bed in the hospital. A seventy-two hour hold and five refused phone calls from my father. I didn't want him to hurt, I didn't want my mom to be disappointed that I was still alive.

I lived with Jordan for a while, in an apartment full of milk crate furniture and stale food. The living was easy and pressure-free so I had to run away. Off and out to a destruction I was familiar with. Rattling my insides, hoping by some will my soul would just abort itself and save me the tubes and IV's.

I had received a call from him after my dad passed, someone must have let him know. "I'm so sorry for your loss Rory, come out for a visit. I know how much your father meant to you."

I straightened the books on my coffee table, kicking the pile underneath with my clumsy well-meaning feet. Gregory Corso, Allen Ginsberg, William Burroughs. I read about the Beats religiously, with a sickness of desperation. The breaking apart of convention was something that played well with the tune of my mind. Sometimes if things were quiet for more than a few moments I thought I could hear Kerouac warning me about the gruesome ways my organs could turn inside out if I kept on the way I was.

Most days I didn't get drunk on purpose. I forgot about the floor beneath me and was dumping alcohol down my throat before I even realised I was awake. Once the first few sips were down I only needed more so I could reach some point of forgetfulness that felt safe.

I could always read no matter how drunk I got. I felt the words swimming and growing inside me. I let poetry move in with me and I dreamt of songs that I couldn't hear.

Chuck would get it, without ever having said so I knew he understood me. There was an exchange between us and our broken cowardliness that I kept now in the sleeves of my chest. It was the way he spoke to me. He didn't judge me and he didn't discard my opinion. He really listened to me for free. Hadn't felt that way since I had Jordan in my life. We'd talk loosely for hours, transcending the need to make sense or stay on a continuous thought.

Friends like that don't come often, and I fucked up the first one so maybe now the universe was granting me a second chance. I could do something right; I could let someone in.

I got to the liquor store in a frenzy, parked diagonally across two spots and dragged my body to the door. My hands shook and my skin felt vacuum sealed. A few stumbly rage-aching paces around the store and I squinted my eyes to block out the bright fluorescents, keeping one closed while I searched for a bottle. Crown Royal, Jack Daniels, Wisers. Crown Royal, Jack Daniels, Wisers. I had been drinking Jack when I met Chuck so I picked it off the shelf as a toast.

Counter is sticky and crusty, and the man behind it smiles at me like he knows me.

"Good to see you again."

I pull the money out of my pocket, crinkled with sweat, I try to pull the bills apart but my fingers fall off them at every trembling shake.

"Should you be driving?"

"Yep."

He bags my bottle. "You been drinking yet tonight?"

"Not enough."

He tries to make eye contact with me. I dodge him, irritated at this attempt to connect. "Thanks man."

"Hey dude, wait a minute," he says.

I roll my eyes so far back in my head I'm afraid they'll get stuck. "What?"

He looks at me, eyebrows so far down his forehead they interfere with his eyelashes. "You sure you're not drunk?" He feels guilty for selling me booze, it's written all over him. If I die in a car crash he'll feel personally responsible for the rest of his pathetic life.

"Fuck off." I walk out the door, curse the tingling bell. Mental note never to go to that liquor store again. I drive out as fast as possible in case that fucker calls the cops. I have my phone on the dash playing The Kinks out of shitty, tinny speakers. My sister calls and interrupts Lola. I'm pissed off. Swerving through traffic as I avoid her calls. I sing loudly like it'll make her go away. My house isn't far from the liquor store and I'm guzzling booze before I've locked my car doors. Singing Temptation by New Order, feeling the denial party set in my mind.

"Shut the fuck up, you loaded douche." Someone yells from their balcony.

I flip them off and let a belch rip through my facehole.

"Disgusting asshat."

The people in this building hate me. I mean loathe me. I've had the cops buzz me more than I can remember. Sometimes the same ones show up and they look exhausted as soon as they see me. I take great pride in this. They never take me away because I'm always about ready to pass out by the time they show up and can't remember what noise I made anyways, so I agree to keep it down.

Angela is still calling me but I'm content in the armchair of my intoxication. Chuck walks around my head in circles. Jordan joins him at each interval and I feel warm. Not such a piece of shit after all, I could possibly be made to exist well in the presence of these strong people that accept me. I forget sometimes that Jordan isn't in my life anymore. I can instantaneously go back to a place where he was around all the time and encapsulate myself in our past together. I can dance and swim in it for hours if I let everything else melt away.

Eight missed calls now and four voicemails. I could feel my sister's frantic worry. She wanted too badly for me to be a different person than the one I was. I wished she'd mind her own business and let me do what I need to get through the day. Not all of us can be so well-to-do as she is. Angela clutches ideals the way that most of us never learn how. By the eleventh grade she already had universities pinned down and a growing correspondence with the deans. She was accepted into people's lives and histories by default, just because she was a lovely person to know. She rarely laughed or made light of anything. She had a way of talking to you like she already knew what you were going to say and why. The poise my sister displayed was inspiring to me only insofar as I wished I had a fraction of her stability.

Ever since childhood she was the one who looked out for me the most. She noticed that I always needed extra and while this exasperated my mother and filled her with more distress and frustration than one person should ever know, Angela always took the liberty of making sure I was okay because she knew someone had to. Mom on the other hand only wanted me around when things seemed to be going well, but she could never meet my eye or look at me with a straight, un-aggravated expression. I couldn't blame her but I tried to make things easier. I tried to disappear through the cracks in her, tried to not show up too much.

The more disorderly I got the more she grieved me existing at all. There was a time in my childhood where it seemed she felt something almost like love for me. I found out it was a lie and made a pact with myself to disappear every chance I got. I felt guilty every time she had to look at me.

My sister never gave up on me though, even when I left everyone in the dark wondering if I was dead or alive. I think I was solely responsible for the bulk of her panic attacks. She only seemed to have them at the thought of something happening to me. I could hear her voice now, as she tried to call me, working hard to catch her breath and stay calm for my benefit. I never went back home after I left Jordan's. I kept hold of my family by only a thin, fraying piece of thread that Angela held the reins to. My dad held me together as I tried to roll away. My mom let me go before I had even left.

When we were little kids, Angela's rabbit died. She told my parents she knew what to do and that we had to have a funeral and move on. She organised the whole thing, made programs and compiled music to play. My parents tried not to laugh, but I was struck by the whole thing. I was not yet ready to face mortality, especially the way my sister faced it: with a fearless urgency to get past it. The same thing did not happen when my father died. None of us wanted to get past it because it wasn't supposed to happen. We never envisioned a life where he would not exist. And now things with her just weren't the same.

The three of us would hang out sometimes sans mom because she never wanted to join us. We got along really well and I imagined sometimes that our family was just us three. I'm not sure if Angela ever knew the truth. I don't know if she knew what reasons I had to hate myself or why mom didn't love me. She never let it show if she did. She and dad always had a way of treating me like I wasn't a freak, though I know in my true form I would never fit into their family. The seamlessness that strung their conversations together was something I had to fight to have with anyone. I spent most of my time stuffed into books. Places where I could see self-loathing actualised without having to reflect on who I was or the presence of it in me. I drank to make the things in my head go away, but they never truly shut up.

I watched Angela call and call and call and I could feel her concern in my own throat, unswallowable. I wished she didn't worry about me so much. At times I enjoyed it because I wanted out of my self-pity but most often, I felt it was useless and she should move on with her life. It'd be better for her if she'd stop trying to save me. I really thought I'd convinced her of that the last time I saw her, at dad's funeral. But here she was again and I think she knew that now more than ever I needed not to be left alone. It's a strange thing really, when you don't want to be alone but you have no idea how to be around anyone. It's like this ugly sound hangs around and between you and everyone and gets in the way of making any progress in speech. Besides being worn out by myself, I felt my tongue would swell and close my throat up if I did try to tell her how I was feeling, and what would I say anyways? It was my fault that dad was dead. I may as well have killed him. Just by existing I turned the things around me to rot. I should have taken it into my own hands that she and I talk again, but I had no guts to talk to her since my dad's funeral.

The edges were melting now, guilt subsiding and resting my grief self and my guilt self in a shadow behind my drunk self. Quiet, quiet, quiet.

Chapter Seven

Crisp morning air, hanging death on its clothesline, waiting for someone to break through its thin cords. I watched the procession from a distance. The funeral was held outside as my dad would have wanted. He loved the outdoors, the way the air would 'wash materialistic preoccupations from his skin.' My mom said she loved the outdoors but she rarely went outside. We all have our reasons for being afraid of the world. I could hear the breaking apart of the guests. The cracking of their faces. I felt like a fool, standing in the trees, the only place I felt comfortable grieving. I don't even know what I'd say if I had been invited.

I was made to stand apart from everyone, living the funeral only through my dysfunctional imagination. I felt like I wasn't allowed to love my dad as much as I did. If my mom saw me at the funeral, she might be the next one in the ground.

Hallelujah played through a strong speaker, the original version. My dad loved Leonard Cohen. That song was already haunted with a thousand griefs and longings but now it would forever match the shade of my father's absence.

I wasn't invited to his funeral, and why would I have been? The last time I set foot in my parents' house, it was made abundantly clear that 50% of them wanted nothing to do with my being there. Today was different though. Thinking I had earned the right to be there could have been selfish, but is it selfish to want the opportunity to honour someone you loved? If I did it improperly, no one was more sorry than I was, and no one taught me what I could have done better. Looking back on all the times I shared with my dad and all the ways I took him for granted made me fractionally happy that I wasn't invited. I could imagine the look on my mom's face if she had to invite me, but the only person who might have been able to convince her to was the reason for the event after all.

Angela was wearing a blue dress while everyone else wore black, always the optimist. She came to sit next to me on a grassy hill down away from the cemetery. The funeral procession was still going on behind us but she must have felt that I deserved to be a part of it as well.

"Hey, Ror. Why don't you come up and say hello to everyone?"

"Why?"

"Come on, stop being self-loathing. Mom would be happy to see you."

"Please don't tell me you believe that, listen to how hard she's crying now that I'm here." Normally Angela was the level-headed one, she saw things the way that they were and viewed them at face value with ease. She wasn't overly emotional or quick to react.

"She's not crying because of you. She doesn't even know you're here."

We sat in silence, the exact things I wanted to say to her lost in it. The breeze around us was so loud I felt my head swell, taking me somewhere I wasn't ready to go.

"I miss him."

"I know. I know you do."

We sat there allowing the silence between us to grow larger and larger until our spirits floated completely away from each other. In the span of fifteen minutes, I could feel myself being eradicated from our sibling bond. Where we should have been consoling each other in our mutual loss, there was only stillness and a bored sense of disgust.

"Come on, please come with me. You deserve to be there as much as anyone."

"I wasn't invited. I spent my whole childhood

being somewhere I wasn't wanted. I'm not doing that to her now."

"She wants you there. She just didn't know how to say it."

"That's a load of bullshit and you know it. If she wanted me there, she would have found a way to say it. But she didn't."

"Not everything is about you. She just lost the love of her life, Rory. Please don't make this another chance to feed your insecurities."

"If you actually believe that she wants me there, you're way stupider than I thought you were."

She paused for a minute, and I thought for sure I'd crossed a line, that this time she would be done with me. "I know if you just tried, you could fix the things between you. I don't know why you guys act this way around each other."

"Yeah, that's right, you don't know. So stop pretending that we can fix something that you don't know anything about."

"Can we go somewhere after this is done? Talk a little? I miss you."

I pulled a flask from my inside pocket and swallowed my I-miss-you-too. I knew I was provoking her. I wanted her to leave me alone and force me to stay with her simultaneously. Just as predicted, Angela grabbed the flask from my hand. A loss of will let her take it from me. I watched it soar down the hill we were sitting on. I breathed deep trying to suck the sprays of alcohol from the air before facing her.

"You are not doing this shit again Rory."

"Seems like I am." Sometimes I thought it might be easier for people if they hated me.

"Why are you doing this? You're so much better than this." I felt a twinge of guilt doing this to her at her father's funeral.

"No I'm not actually better than this. You say this shit out of some sort of familial obligation. You don't know anything about me. I'm not a fucking good person, Angela. I'm not better than this, I am this."

"So you're giving up on yourself?"

"I guess you could call it that if there was anything to give up on. I'm just living up to my potential."

"Why are you laughing? Rory, this isn't funny. You're destroying your life, why are you so selfish? You wonder why mom doesn't want to be around you. It's because you keep pulling this shit and we can't just put our lives aside to clean up yours all the time."

"See, there you go. You don't understand how selfless it is for me to destroy myself like this. You have no fucking clue why mom doesn't want me around. Why don't you just go take care of your kids instead of projecting all your unhappiness on me? You can't fix me. You can't do a goddamn thing about it."

"You're being completely unreasonable."

"No I'm not, you are. Stop coming to try and convince me that mom loves me and all this crap. She doesn't and neither do you, because if you did love me, you'd leave me the fuck alone."

"Rory, seriously fuck you." She got up to leave. I knew she was really angry because that's the only time she ever swore. I grabbed her arm and for one moment in the bulk of all my mistakes I wanted to say something like sorry. I wanted to say something that would help her understand why I hated my ties to our mother's womb, instead I said: "Stop trying to help me, Ange."

"What choice do I have? You're a lost cause."

Chapter Eight

I stood on the street, dialling my sister's number over and over again. She'd just called me eight times, but now she wasn't picking up. I got more frantic every time I heard her voicemail. When she finally answered, it shattered me.

"Rory?" I hadn't picked up my sister's calls in weeks. When I told her to stop taking care of me I didn't mean abandon me. She never ceased trying to reach out, and my own lack of reciprocation flung back at me and projected onto her. I was hollowing people's chests and blaming them for the emptiness.

"Angela. Why don't you fucking care about me? Nobody cares about me." I grabbed a fist full of my hair and sat down on the curb, rocking my head between my legs.

"Rory, what's going on?" She sounded like she'd been sleeping.

"You're the one who called me."

"Are you drunk?"

"No." I moaned into the phone.

"You're drunk, Rory. Please, can I come get you?" The sharp inhale of fear. John in the background: Hang up on him Ange, I'm trying to sleep. Fuck's sake. Her husband never wanted her to take care of me. From an outside perspective, I was a hopeless blood sucking waste. He hated me but she didn't care. I never told her I loved her for that.

My mouth closed and opened, words flying from somewhere far away and unknown. "I don't want to see you, I don't want to see anybody. Just bring dad back. Why the fuck did he leave me like this?"

"Rory, please listen to me."

"Fuck you." I threw my phone into the street, triggering another moan from the alien voice. The anger in my spirit was making me high. I punched the back window of my shitty car, felt the glass crack and watched the blood trickle down my arm before I felt the pain, radiating with the rhythm of my blood flowing, throwing sharps, throttling my forearm.

I watched transfixed as the blood pooled in the crease of my elbow. The parts that dried made blotted tree branches of my skin. Listening to the sounds of the car alarm ring in my ears, knowing damn well I could turn it off at any time, I lay down on the cool pavement, allowing the contour of the man-made earth to bruise my bony body with its harsh structure. Somehow everything felt really quiet. I was alone. Completely alone with the blood pooling near my arm and the screams of violated steel.

"Excuse me sir, can you stand up?"

I lifted my head and squinted into the rising sun in his hand. I covered my face and fell back down. "Nah."

He stood over me, a second pair of footsteps trailing tentatively behind him. He shone the flashlight in my face and then on the car that was still screaming. "You know whose car this is?"

"Yeah dude, it's my car. Everything's fine here. I'm trying to sleep." I banged on my chest to try to get my heart to beat harder, pump blood back into my legs so I could fuck off.

"So what's happened to your hand?"

I lifted it into the air to show him and shrugged.

"You vandalised a vehicle. You've caused a public disturbance. Stand up."

"No thanks."

The second pair of footprints climbed closer to my head until they were right next to me. I felt a shudder through my whole body as a boot made contact with my bloody hand. Next thing, I was clutching the damned useless thing to my chest sitting upright. The officers took this opportunity to grab me under my armpits, my legs betraying me once again, falling into their clutch. I kicked at them with my flailing limbs.

"Listen, you entitled little shit. You're coming down to the station. We'll decide what to do with you when we get there."

I started laughing. I was forced against the hood of my car. I laughed even harder, tears assaulting my face, completely aware that I was starting to lose it and that I reeked of booze and would be held responsible for my actions. I was afraid of how little I felt I could control myself.

The police officer cuffed me and dragged me into the back of the car. I felt safe behind that piece of plexiglass that separates the front seats from the back. "You're both incompetent pieces of shit. You know that? Cowardly power-tripping cunts. Fuck you both. I hope you choke on your own pride. You stupid, shallow, worthless assholes. You're incompetent and power hungry."

"Save your breath kid, you're making things a lot worse for yourself the more you talk like that." He kept his voice even.

I was miserable and afraid. I felt I had nothing to lose but I was trying to dig for things that I could just willingly give up. I wanted to lose. I wanted to accentuate my pain so that it felt justified. I looked out the window and waited to be taken anywhere but where I'd just been.

This ended up being a putrid room, lined with benches, a break in them where a steel toilet sat vacant and cold. There was only one other person in there and I watched him stir on the floor where he sat ripping at his fingernails with his teeth. He watched me, rabid and dog-like, his lips freckled with blood.

I looked at him for a little too long I guess, because he shouted at me, spit spraying from his teeth. "Fuck off, gooch."

Gooch? Whatever. I wasn't in the mood to listen to some kid's ignorant shit. I didn't even have the capacity to respond. He had dirty blond hair, flying in all directions trying to run from the madness contained in the skull beneath it. Dark eyes, full moons intoxicated in their centres. His face was covered in what I hoped was dirt and he was wearing an undershirt with stains on it, holes in all of his clothes.

The smell of the cell was foul, and it didn't take me long to realise why. My counterpart was pointing at a heaping, steaming pile of shit in the middle of the floor. "You see that? You see that?"

I nodded at him, doing everything in my power to avoid opening my mouth, avoid tasting the air.

"That's my shit. You know why I shit on the floor?" He licked the spit and dry blood off his lips. "Cause I'm a fuckin' boss. Alright? Name's Chase. And I'm a fucking boss." He drove his finger into his skinny chest, sneering at me as I stood holding the wall opposite, trying to focus my eyes on him, nodding. He jumped to his feet and grabbed both sides of my face. His breath smelled like cancer, and his eyes were ripened, teeth rotting out of their gums. It was hard to tell how old he was, the closer he got to me.

"You see that toilet over there? You shit in that toilet, cause you're not the boss. Alright? I'm the boss so I shit on the floor. You're not the boss so you shit on the toilet." He backed off quickly as though something had been resolved, nodding in agreement with himself, clapping his hands together. He knelt toward the floor, holding eye contact until he was hunched right next to the toilet.

I shook my head and looked out at the walls and the bars that held me in. No more interesting of a place than the lecture halls at school. I sighed and rested myself back against the wall, slinking down like Chase had and trying to ignore the stinking mound of feces on the floor that sat between us.

"So, why are you here?"

"Fuck off, I told you I'm a boss."

"Okay."

Silence followed this. I watched Chase as he muttered incoherent things under his breath. I was faintly aware of my heart beating in its own separate drunk tank. A nervousness sat with me that I hadn't lived with since Jordan picked me up at the hospital, concerned and quiet.

"I'm fucking drunk." Chase laughed at me, as though we were old buddies. I was afraid to laugh with him but I smiled. The way he looked at me made the smell of the shit on the floor five times as potent.

He passed out very shortly after that. I started shaking, a chill tracing my spinal column, freezing me to the floor.

"I need to get the fuck outta here." I whispered to my knees, scared for the first time I could remember.

Time dragged me through its unrelenting misery. Chase woke periodically to hum to himself, lick his arms, desperate to recycle the poison in his blood. I tried not to watch but couldn't look away, couldn't hold my breath any longer and wondered if the smell of his excrement would become a permanent fixture in my nostrils.

I relived the events of the night in my head over and over again trying to turn them from one thing to another. I never yelled at my sister like that. She always was a pillar to me, even when she irritated me with her damned positive outlook on everything.

I was in her house, transcending all need to drink, any need for consumption at all. I allowed her warm hands to push the hair off my face and felt a cold compress on my forehead. John decided he could trust me after all. Angela's children suddenly loved me and surrounded me with their youth, giving it to me in little gifts wrapped in laughter. Jenny and Connor. Their preciousness filled me with contrition and all my longings slipped away from my fingers. I managed to keep food down. I managed a laugh and even a healthy cry. Angela and I sat and talked through the night, past the children running themselves out of energy and John removing himself from a conversation he didn't want to understand. I finally told my sister the truth and she accepted it easily. I slept on her couch and woke to the sound of my skin shrinking to fit my body. Everything was contentment and I didn't have to be afraid anymore. There was finally a person with hands strong enough to help me hold the misfortunes of my life.

Watching Chase sleep, I couldn't shake the on-edge feeling of being stuck in a room alone with him. Unpredictable people scared me more than anything. I didn't like not knowing what was happening or what could happen. I was addicted to control. Sitting in there, I felt like I had lost it, and that was worse than any amount of feces that I could have to accustom my nostrils to.

On hour three of tasting his shit in my mouth, I started to really give up on comfort. I felt micro-epiphanies engulf me, where I thought that being in here was an extremely sound way of being forced to gather my thoughts, but then they'd just as quickly slip away and I'd feel sorry for myself again, wondering what the logic was behind ever thinking even for a moment that this predicament was meaningful.

I chased myself around the idea of never drinking again. What a joke that would be. I swallowed the thought and tasted my tongue, coated in apprehension and avoidance. How ironic, now I'd have to call my sister back. I hated asking her for help, because sometimes it felt like she was sitting there waiting for it all the time. She was so eager and I didn't deserve half of that kind of anticipation about my well-being. One of the arresting officers came back and told me I could make a phone call. He seemed way less excited about kicking me through the mud, tired and nearing the end of his shift. He held eye contact with the shit on the ground and sighed, "Chase, you gotta stop shitting on the floor. Every fucking weekend buddy."

"Hey, Ange, I need you to pick me up." I felt resigned as I said it.

"Where are you? Are you okay? Are you hurt? Where are you?"

"Yeah, I'm at the police station. The one downtown, could you come soon?"

"Rory, what the hell? What happened?"

"Nothing. Just please come get me." I spoke through my teeth. It was hard not to lose patience with the people who loved me when I knew without them, I could have a lonely chaotic life and a peaceful early grave.

"I'm on my way."

I hung up. I didn't know how to say thank you to my sister. The thought of her left a lump in my throat that was hard to breathe through. She dropped her life countless times to clean up mine. I knew that leaving her kids to save their good-for-nothing uncle over and over again was either giving them a hero complex to grow into or severe emotional abandonment issues. Two sides of the same psychiatric pad.

The officer walked away to talk to his partner again, leaving me alone with the foul smell of Chase. Suddenly, I had to take a shit. I could feel the familiar gurgling in my stomach, the cramping that couldn't be ignored, the tightening and loosening of the sphincter as it threatened you to do it with or without your help, music in my gut. I looked down at Chase, asleep, holding the toilet bowl. How could I shit there now? Some fucking boss he was. Traitorous like the rest of the bosses I'd had in my life. Authoritarian little shit.

I unbuckled my pants and let loose in the corner

of the cell, promoting myself. Chase might have woken up in a stupor thick enough to forget whose shit was whose or if anyone else had even been in there with him. He could still be the boss. What feeble victory he had in his life.

Angela showed up at the exact wrong time to escort me out.

"Jesus, Rory." She was staring wide-eyed at my proud pile of defecation, and me buckling my pants back up wondering why they didn't give us any toilet paper.

She glanced a few times at my swollen hand as she drove us and I thought I could notice her holding her breath.

"I told them about the rough time we've had this year, they seemed to have half a heart in letting you get away with it. But you just can't behave that way, Rory. You just can't do this anymore. I don't know what I'm supposed to do."

"I got it."

"Do you have any idea what you're doing to your life? This isn't funny anymore."

"Can you please stop patronising me? None of this is funny and no one knows that more than I do. Stop acting like I'm completely fucking oblivious to what I'm doing."

"I'm just worried about you." She was trying to meet my eye; I refused each advance. "Do you want to come stay with me awhile? I'm sure you can take a break from school, we can help you get sober."

I started laughing. "I don't want to fucking stop, Ange. I don't want to stop drinking." Tears ripped paths through my face and I couldn't stop them.

"We should really get you some help. You need help. You should get that hand looked at. Can I take you to the hospital? I'm taking you to the hospital."

She always talked in these circles until she answered her own questions. I knew she was grasping at ideas about how to help me. As soon as my father was in the ground, I mentally leased the plot of earth next to him and I didn't know how to stop racing there.

"I'd rather be in a drunk tank than a psych ward, Angela. My drinking isn't even that bad, calm down."

"I'm not going to calm down. I'm not going to stop worrying about you, you're my brother. I can't just sit here and watch you kill yourself and not try to do anything about it." Her voice cracked as she finally began to lose her composure. I knew how hard it was for anyone in my family to have so little certainty about someone they were supposed to be close to. They all knew each other so well, exactly what should be said to whom and when. But I couldn't help who I was, the alien I'd become and had always been.

"You may be worried, but for a few minutes in there I was a fucking boss."

Chapter Nine

Lack of tolerance for my life kept me from buying a new phone since I'd smashed mine in the street. I mean, who could rightfully be bothered keeping in touch with everyone all the time? I thought about Chuck as I itched the bandages on my hand and arm. Thirty-six stitches spread out along the thing, but somehow nothing was broken. The bartender at Tavern had said Chuck was a fixture. I hoped he'd be there tonight to cradle my loneliness with his blunt obscenities.

On my way out to meet my self-loathing, I ran into that human eye roll, Andy.

"Hey." He blew a cloud of strawberry scented douche-vapour in my face. I ignored him. "I'm in your metaphysics class." He added.

"Yeah, I know who you are."

I looked at this guy, his perfect blond hair combed to the side, clothes so expensive it made me wonder what he was doing in an apartment building like mine. "You live here?" I asked him.

"Yeah man, but not for long because I'm a tentative pledge." He sized me up, pointing at me with his unimpressive chest.

"A tentative pledge?"

"Yeah, DKE." He smelled like Hugo Boss frat boy piss and had an entitled way of speaking that led me to wonder how someone so lacking in self-awareness could ever even be considered a tentative frat slog and not instantly promoted to head douchebag.

"Okay, well good luck. See ya."

He laughed as I walked away. Having made no headway with this conversation I searched my head to figure out if it even was one. I arrived at Tavern late that night, unable to go on as sober as I was. Chuck was sitting there half held up by the stool, with his arm slung across the bar counter, one leg on the floor and the other curled under the seat. Relief flooded through me.

"Rory." His lips were covered in thick slobber. Drunk, dribbling speech stuttered out from between them as he happened upon me with unfocused eyes.

"Hey dude, you need a glass of water or something?'

"Fuck water. Whicky."

I winked at the bartender; she placed the water in front of him.

"Take a sip of this, it'll help."

"Help like fuck." It flew across the counter, shattered on the floor, the bottom still intact rolled away. No one seemed to care.

The bartender walked over. The people at Tavern all knew Chuck. They seemed to let things slide in the same way families do. He gave the square foot of bar he lived at life. They didn't seem to mind the space he took up. He was like an extra crack in the paint.

"My boy, don't lose it." His breath reeked of whisky and unwashed teeth, and his tongue sounded like leather moving around in his mouth. He was looking at me in a way I had never been looked at before. Even his eyes didn't seem to want any association with him. They rolled around, searching for a way out.

"Nothing from you tonight. It's my turn to whine. Tired of this clean blowjob from the dirty mouth of society. Fucking cock suck. I should've been granted more. More friendship, irresolute dicks. How hard is it to just hide your fuckin' teeth and show some compassion?" His eyes rolled to meet mine, suddenly stone sober. He took a swig of a new glass of water the bartender had placed in front of him and spat it out. "Fuckin' liver pleasers."

"Anything for you?" She addressed me with a nod.

"I'll get a beer. Whatever's on special."

"It's like chewing on used condoms, tryna get through to them. Their gargling and snarling shit speech. And even after all these years they don't leave me. Rory, you gotta tell me, it ain't like that in your head right?"

"Like what?"

"Murderous, rabid. Fucking stupid." Chuck carried on, tapping his head. "What kinda place is this to live? I can't focus through that bullshit. It's not enough to swallow it down, Rory. It's not enough. Don't tell me you think it'll be enough here for you."

My body tensed into a knot, driving my mind all into one pulsing entity trying to maintain focus. Sober, my eyes blurred listening to the rattling of the tongue that comes around rarely when a man is eclipsed, when his soul passes over the reminiscence of the body's past.

"We gotta get out of here." Chuck was looking around, paranoid. His wild eyes searched the bar for someone he couldn't find. He looked back at me, my uneasiness growing steadily, refusing to plateau. I didn't want to leave with him but my fear gave me no choice.

We paced the block, Chuck stumbling and hitting walls, intentionally or not, I'm unsure. He kept muttering fuck over and over again under his breath like he had forgotten something, or messed something up, or was chasing his brain for a resolution. I followed him to a park, my legs all jellylike and crazy-feeling. I beat them with my fists as we sat down on a bench. I was too sober to deal with all this.

"I gotta tell you something, man." Chuck said to the space next to my ear, looking over my shoulder and then his before crouching next to me. "You can't tell anyone. I gotta disappear, they're back for me. They're coming back all the time."

"Who?"

"The people. My brother. Those little asshole suckers."

I couldn't move my body more than to nod myself into submission under his unsettling talk. He seemed to think what he was saying made sense, so I trusted him that it was going somewhere.

The four of them, they'd done this a dozen times. Dean was the ringleader. He decided who to hit, how and when. He decided when it went too far or not far enough. Lacking empathy wasn't a character flaw in his line of work, but a strength. Graham and Craig followed everything he did because they had never had a chance to be cool before. Dean taught his younger brother Chuck everything he knew. Chuck was too sensitive to let anyone go down alone. And if he got on his brother's good side it limited his beatings at home.

He would have somewhere to be, out of his father's line of fire. They were invincible and lived in the grey area between consequence and justice.

Arnold the crazy cat man, he was easy because he was too afraid to think about himself. Sandra and Bill were going through a divorce. They had bigger things to worry about. Plus, they knew the boys and never would have suspected them. Ted down the block, he had his own record to keep hidden and never would've risked going to the police.

They were victimless crimes so long as they didn't see people as people. Mrs. Sullivan was untouched and seemingly unloved. She was so old that most of her loved ones had not survived the length of her life. "It's obvious she won't miss her shit," Dean said. "She's gonna be gone soon anyway." No one could express the sickness in their guts. Dean invented too many things that were on the line.

Locks were unpickable and Chuck thought this was a sign to reconsider but Dean said only pansy bitches believe in signs so Chuck kept his mouth shut. "We'll break the window." Only the insane mind among them thought this was a rational idea. It was cold outside, and the window broke easily. The shattering barely reverberated through teenage ears, adrenaline guarding them from what they were doing. It can be a protective mechanism, this adolescent hate for the world.

Crawling through the window, one after the other they scrounge around the house looking for things that were worth something to them. Chuck felt an expansion of some void in him. He never liked stuff. He didn't like to own anything because it made him restless, even as a boy. He hated playing with toys because he wanted to be with his mom, and they were always the substitute. He hated robbing people's houses because he just wanted to talk to his brother, but this was always the substitute.

"Sweet dude, check out this cash box."

Of course some elderly people don't believe in having bank accounts, and they trust the world or are reckless or just feel too tired to have anything to lose so they don't lock things up or remember to hide things. There was a wooden box full of money. Dean thought they hit a jackpot and left the realm of serious thought. There was a crash from above their heads that only the other three seemed to care about. Dean was shouting out numbers as he counted the money, growing more and more elated. Chuck's heart sank into a spot he didn't know existed. Everyone was afraid for their own lives but Chuck was afraid for someone else's. There was a screech, and a blur of movements as everyone tried to get out.

Chuck ran upstairs against everyone's protests and cries of: "What the fuck are you doing? You're going to get us caught."

She had collapsed on the stairs. The thinning grey hair caking to her forehead, her breathing unsteady and shallow. She clutched her chest and looked up at Chuck as though he held the cords that connected life and death. The pleading without voice, it crawled under his skin. He yelled for his friends. They came over only to tell him to shut up. "Leave her." Dean's voice was unaffected. He was clutching all her money and a few pieces of jewellery in his greedy dry hands. "Come on, guys. Let's fucking go." Urgency met their ears.

"We have to call an ambulance." Chuck pleaded, the tears on his face were easily mocked by Dean. "We have to, she's dying, she's dying we have to call an ambulance." Dean hit him across the face. Scolded him for caring.

"You wanna go to fucking jail? Leave her, she's an old bat and she was going to die anyways."

"But she's dying now."

"So? She's fucking old. Come on let's get out of here." He was looking into Chuck's face with malice and contempt. "You fucking pussy." That was the last thing Chuck remembered hearing Dean say before he was being dragged out of the house.

All the way home everyone tried to ignore his crying, his relentless tears and sloppy whimpers. He was seventeen years old. He could be tried as an adult, or so he heard from the others. But he didn't care. All he could think about was how he left an old woman to die. On her stairs, in the night. He saw her eyes all the time. He saw her eyes in every face, in every dream, waking or asleep. They were charged with breaking and entering, and incidentally he wasn't tried as an adult after all, so less than a year of his life was occupied by the solitary and relentless task of dragging his body around a disgusting concrete existence, wrapped behind bars, but always more imprisoned by the sound of Mrs. Sullivan choking at his feet.

He never kept in touch with his brother after being released. He never kept in touch with anyone ever again.

"I've never told anyone that. I swallowed it, Rory. I just started chugging it away. You got any booze on you?"

I shook my head, my neck cracked from holding my body so still. "Why are you telling me this?"

"Cause I can tell you're fucked up in the head."

I laughed one loud 'Ha' into the silence of the park. I thought of telling him my story, the ways I'd disturbed the order of things. My throat itches at the idea. The park was sobering us up as the leaves fell from the trees, threatening winter in the cold dark of night. A trickle of doom rolled down my spine and numbed my legs. I wanted to leave, run, hide. I didn't want to be stuck here sitting with a man who had more guilt under his belt than one person could take. It made me sick, cold, tired, like my bones were asleep and I'd never catch up to wake them.

Chuck slapped me on the back. "You live around here, kid?"

"No," I lied. I couldn't meet his eye. His story left me with a lingering death in my skin that I didn't need hanging around.

"Hmm."

"I should head out though, I gotta go to school in the morning."

"School? Still?"

"Yeah, there's this thing about school where it keeps happening no matter how much you want it to stop."

"Sounds like a choice to me."

His advice wasn't wanted by me. Welcome. Or invited. My legs wiggled in the sockets of my knees, trying to urge me to escape him. I couldn't move despite their persistence.

"I should get outta here anyway. Come back around to see me whenever." He briefly squeezed my shoulder.

"Yeah, okay."

He walked away, doing a dance with his legs. Unleashing some freedom at spewing his shit story through his lips. Where did he get off thinking I could hold that kinda shit? I was sober for the first time in weeks and I felt too many of my body parts interacting with each other. I couldn't escape the reiteration of his words through my head. The strange parallels between us. I never wanted to see him again, to feel this sick dissociated fear. The rattling of my heart. The strong magnetic pull I felt to him. He had rolled the words off his inebriated tongue so smoothly they tucked me into a trance and made the rest of the world look wacked out and distorted once he stopped talking.

I couldn't see him again. Had to see him again. Hated my weird drive to know people I had no business being around. He let an old woman die. But in a lot of ways his crimes were comparable to mine. Young, youthful, naive, doe-eyed crimes.

I watched him walk himself out of my sight, losing myself in his silhouette and the fading echo of his feet on the crunching leaves. The night sucked me into it and I paced around the block for forty-five minutes, frozen in moments from someone else's past.

I woke up late the next evening having slept through all of my classes, the same ones I missed every day that week, and headed back out to the bar. I hadn't drunk anything the night before, not even the shitty cheap beer I paid for. My veins were shrivelling up in my arms, body itchy and dry. I drank down a glass of water, ate a piece of stale bread with old crusty butter on it, took two Advil and headed out.

Chuck wasn't there today, which relieved me. I didn't want to ever run into him again. I didn't want to hear about his shit. I wanted insight. I wanted to be around people who could help me better myself. I sat drinking alone. It tasted less sharp and all my senses seemed a little hazy.

I thought a lot about what he said the night before and felt a loneliness in my throat that I couldn't swallow. I looked at the stool he normally occupied. Why did I ever think that some stranger could save me? Why did I even think there was anything redeemable about me, or anyone else for that matter?

Claire wasn't working that night. The new bartender was strikingly beautiful. I searched my head for where I knew her from. She was in my Plato class. She'd sit next to me sometimes and try to strike up a conversation. She had a soft, raspy voice. I stared at her when I thought she wasn't looking. I thought of fucking her to gain some grander release from my pity but I couldn't make my fantasy go further than licking the skin on her neck. She caught me looking, walked over to me and started wiping the clean patch of counter that separated us and I felt ashamed.

"Hey, your name's Rory right? You're in my Plato class."

"That'd be it."

"I love that name— it rolls nicely off the tongue." She leaned over to look at me. Flirting effortlessly. I caught a glimpse of the crease of her breast for the second I let my eyes wander. My heart hammered where it wasn't located and I yearned for touch more than I'd ever wanted a drink. I could smell her perfume. "And what's your name?"

"I'm Calla."

"Calla. Beautiful name."

"It's Greek. My parents are American but they try to be trendy." She flushed and looked at the ground. "So do you need another drink?"

"Oh yeah, yeah that'd be great."

She came back with it and looked at me nervously. "Can I be a bit forward with you?"

"Yeah, sure."

"I think you're hot as hell. I get off at two tonight and if that's not late for you and you're around, I wouldn't mind rolling your name off my tongue a few more times."

Heat rose up my chest and caressed my face. "We'll see about that then. I might be around." She was beautiful in a hard way, half the joy of looking at her was reading her face, finding a new form of beauty every time you looked at it.

"Just in case you're not around, here's my number." She slid a napkin across the bar. She turned her back to me and I caught myself thinking too hard about the place my heart was beating now. Bile rose into my throat. I threw my drink back and decided to carry on at home, where I could think about her without having to commit to anything. Whisky warmed my chest as I looked back at her, unable to fight the itch in me like I needed her. Her confused and slightly hurt expression lingered in my memory as I realised I'd left her phone number on the bar.

On the way home I walked myself over and over through the ways she'd turned me on, ashamed of my sexual sobriety. I'd never been with anyone before and though I yearned now to begin, I had to abstain from sex. I was too much of a coward with my body. Even when I tried to masturbate, I couldn't tell if I was puking or cumming. Every organ seized up at the touch of another. The only girlfriend I'd ever had eventually left me for making her feel unlovable. I had nothing worthwhile to offer anyone.

Chapter Ten

The world was way too much for me. Couldn't even really open my blinds. I felt like everyone wanted something from me that I didn't have to give. If I could find out why that weird man had told me what he told me, maybe I could rid myself of whatever had inspired him to do it. Chuck let an old woman die, why was that my problem? God, I needed a drink. I was supposed to be in class. I decided to make myself breakfast instead. I had one egg in my fridge and a loaf of bread. I took a few slices that weren't mouldy, fried the egg and made a disgusting, soggy sandwich.

My body was so surprised at having food stuffed into it that it wanted to celebrate by cleaning my entire apartment. I sat down on my couch when I got sick of picking up after myself and stared at the wall where most people might have a mounted flat screen.

I picked up a book and tried to read it but my thoughts kept overpowering the words on the page. Chuck was such a bloody weirdo, why would I ever care about seeing him again? And especially today, right after he'd told me what he told me. I needed time to process that shit too. I also needed a drink, and to stop staring at the walls of my apartment. I couldn't stomach the thought of going outside. I couldn't stomach the thought of the sun illuminating everything around me. Lights and sounds and presences of other people.

I had to get out to the bar but when I left my apartment the fall sun felt too hot. It was only five degrees and I was sweating. I tucked my notebook under my arm, carried it with me when I felt afraid of myself, in case I had to let parts of me leak out, in case it all got to be too much to carry. Maybe I did want to see Chuck again, to know if the night was real or if it had been a figment of my imagination. Everything blurred together on the sidewalk. I could see the face of Mrs. Sullivan, eyes wide and lifeless. I wanted to know if she was okay in death, if death brought anyone a sense of peace or relief. If any of the guilt that she felt in her life now lived in Chuck, I wanted to know.

I walked around the block maybe five times. I had lost an hour of time thinking about Chuck, fearing Chuck, feeling like a strange thing was moving through my body, telling me that if I didn't find him I would slowly go insane.

My school work was eating at me. I had so many missed deadlines that I didn't care about. I found myself standing outside of Tavern. It was three o'clock in the afternoon so maybe he wouldn't even be there, but I couldn't risk going inside and finding him sitting at that bar stool like he had all those times before. I walked over to the park where we'd sat together and he told me about the thing that would haunt him for the rest of his life.

I walked back around the block, started to head back to my house, paced up and down and up and down and found myself sitting on the edge of the sidewalk panicking. Every time someone told me something about their life that caused them pain I thought of their stories as if I was remembering my own life. I felt like I was Chuck. I wasn't solidified in myself enough yet to take people in, I would have to face the possibility of becoming them and having to live with all their guilt and remorse and bad memories.

I spat on the ground and walked to a liquor store. Got a bottle in a brown paper bag and tried to walk back to my apartment but couldn't make it very far.

I sat down in the alley behind the liquor store, I needed a moment to get ahold of myself. I sat pouring myself onto the page, unable to hold anything in, barely able to write legibly enough for any of it to make sense. My hand throbbed every time I bent my stitched-up fingers. The pain made it hard to focus on what I was trying to let out. Not sure if the words were flowing articulately, I took gulps from the bottle, hoping no one would find me there. Hoping I could have some peace and just find these moments to come undone, let some of it go. Take the weight off.

Was she eighty years old? Ninety? Am I focusing enough on my own life? Am I already eighty years old only remembering what it felt like to be twenty-five? Who will I be when I'm eighty? When I'm ninety? Will I even be alive then? People flick by my eyes like ashes on a burning coast, melting in the shore. I don't want to think about the people I've known or the way my hands shake when I try to let them out. I wish that I had some way to express all the grief that sits in me but it's not mine and so I have no way to name it. If there was a single other person who ever felt this way I wouldn't know how to talk to them. It is all too much, sharing experience. All the same, so is solitude. I don't know a single other person who has felt as empty as me because I can't stomach listening to them.

If this is a normal part of the human experience I want to know, when does the ride end? And how many times will I throw up once I get off? People say that you can't be brave if you haven't felt fear, but if we never felt fear, we wouldn't need to be brave in the first place, so what's the point? Everything is an echo of something else.

How can anyone really measure or prove how fast or slow the time moves? The good days race by and the bad ones drag on. Are we just playing like we've forgotten how it hurts to be young?

I don't know if anything I say makes any sense, I sure as hell know that it doesn't make sense to me.

If I am anything at all, I am lost.

I don't know how many ways I can carry this out anymore. Why isn't there a single person in this world who can show me that what I am isn't so damned and ugly?

Chapter Eleven

Dad was always working, as far as I knew. He was around less and less as I got older. As the years dragged by, it felt like he wanted little to do with me. I don't blame him for the distance. If I could have escaped myself, I would've gone too. Even when I had no clue how to be a tolerant person I still thought of those times when I was young, when he'd accept me in his space like I belonged there.

When he wasn't away at the office, I used to love helping my dad peel potatoes in the kitchen. When I was a child I was slow, but he had so much patience back then. He didn't rush me or yell at me, he just wanted me to make sure I didn't get hurt. There was the one time I sliced my finger so bad cutting carrots I had to get stitches. He took me to the hospital and made me feel brave even with snot and tears covering my face.

"Hey, Roy." Andy snapped me out of my reverie. "Did you know that throats are just face assholes and puke is just face shit?" I could hear his friend laughing next to him.

The class was a small one. Probably thirty-five students, half of which never showed up. One of the smaller lecture classes, which I liked because being around a lot of people in the same room made it too stuffy to think. "Pssst. Roy." Apparently this was very funny to Andy. He and his friend kept whispering about me and I tried not to notice. Andy had no integrity. I felt no obligation to respond. I was empty of identity after all, and wouldn't respond even if they'd called me by the right name.

"Dad. What's your middle name?" I always had a piece of paper next to me at the kitchen table at breakfast. Writing down fun facts that came into my head. From an early age I had a drive to find out as much as I could about where I came from.

"Rory, don't talk with your mouth full, please. My middle name is Allan."

"So, your name is Dad Allan Langford?" I started scribbling it down.

My mother gave my father a silent, endearing look. "Your dad's name isn't dad."

My heart dropped. "What is it then?"

"His name is Patrick. "

"Wait, does that mean your name isn't mom?" I felt cheated. Although this was a fact many children my age had to learn, in the moment it was the ultimate betrayal.

"No. My name is Joyce."

"But then why do I have to call you mom and dad?" I was upset, and confused.

My dad was trying not to laugh at that point. I could hear him clanking around in the kitchen shortly after. The best way to hide your face and your reaction is to turn your back and leave the room. Joyce crouched down beside me and put on her rare tender voice. Mothers had a better way of not laughing right at you.

"Because we are your parents, sweetie. That's who we are. Mom and dad." Her smile flinched on her face, quickly painted back on as she too turned away to hide some expression I didn't yet understand.

***

"Fuck yo, is he crying?" Whispering now. "What a pussy."

I turned around to meet his mocking laughter. "What the fuck do you want?"

"Come to our party tomorrow night."

"Nah, I'm good." I turned back around and tried to focus on what the professor was saying. Metaphysics, the meaning of meanings. What it all means underneath what we think it means. The what is and what was and what could be. The enchanting afterthought, clutched between a fist and suckled and milked for recognition. What is reality, what is the nature of reality? Blah, blah, blah.

"Man, come on."

"Why is dad always late coming home?" I asked myself this every day, but my mom only once.

"He'll be home soon." Adults never answered the questions you asked them. As though they think that you can't handle the truth. Turns out, this youth is the only time that you can handle the truth without taking everything personally.

"But why isn't he home now?"

"Rory, he's working." My mom was always exhausted back then. She no longer crouched beside me and asked how I was doing or made any attempt to comfort me when she already knew that the answer wasn't ideal. I slumped back into my chair. My stupid hair falling into my stupid eyes. Mom immediately combed it back to the side where it presumably belonged. She seemed to care more about my appearance than my feelings. The less my dad was around, the more my mom wanted to hide the way our lives charred and burned. She didn't want anyone to believe how little she loved me, even me. But I could feel it, even then. She hardly looked at me unless to fix me up.

"Rory?"

The whole class was staring at me. My chin was shaking. I was tearing the edge of my textbook, whimpering softly but loud in the context of the room. I hadn't realised when the split occurred between realities then and now, or that so many eyes were on my vulnerability. I nodded to the professor as composed as I could.

"Yeah, what?"

"Do you know the meaning of conceptualism?"

"That concepts have no substantial basis in reality and only exist concretely in the mind?"

"That's a good observation, does anyone else have anything to add to that?" He cautiously moved his eyes from my face and scanned the rest of the room. The silence was thick, taunting, vigilant.

When no one said anything he looked back at the clock, five minutes still left. "You may all go now. I'll look forward to reading your essays next week. Have a good weekend. "

People were filing out quickly. Most of them had been anticipating this part of the class for the last hour and fifteen minutes. "Mr. Langford, can I please speak with you for a minute? It's not mandatory, I just want to check up on you. You haven't seemed yourself."

"Sorry."

"No need to be sorry. I just noticed you haven't been participating much, and you haven't handed in the last two assignments."

See, all these people really cared about was how you were doing on your essay, how well your brain was working so you could become a farm animal for the rest of society to feast on. Fucking manufactured intelligence created in a bubble. I wanted to tell him to fuck off but that came from a different part of myself that I didn't like being acquainted with, after all I liked what's-his-name.

"I promise I'm fine."

"Okay, well if there's anything you need to talk about let me know. I can set you up with counselling services or offer you an extension if you need it."

"Well, my dad died but I don't need an extension. I'm fine." I already had one extension rotting in my gut.

Professor Blankedy-Blank's face sucked the blood back into his body. "I'm so sorry for your loss."

"Yeah but I'm fine, see you next week."

I left, knowing if I stayed any longer he'd try to help me or encourage me. I didn't have time for that.

I didn't need his help. What I needed was for people to get off my back and let me grieve and heal the way I was going to. The way I knew how, which was isolation and booze.

Just like a middle school nightmare, Andy and his friend were waiting outside the classroom door. Andy's friend was quite a lot shorter than him. He had a face like a pug but looked down on everyone somehow despite his height. He stood with his legs way further apart than was probably necessary. He had a hat on backwards, a tuft of hair sticking out the front part and balanced on his head like he had tightened it too much and forgot how to loosen it. Andy was wearing a white shirt and a white ball cap with a white jean vest. His shoes matched his shirt as well, white Pumas with gold on the quarter. It was obvious just from looking at him that his life's mission was to be part of a frat.

"Come to our party tomorrow." Andy was standing uncomfortably close to me. His friend made an ugly sound that some might have considered a laugh.

"Nah, I'm good." Andy pushed a piece of paper

into my hand. It was a handmade flyer for a frat party.

"Thanks but I won't be there."

"Dude, there's free booze."

"I don't need your dad's breast milk."

I walked away, didn't feel the courtesy of goodbye was something these nimrods deserved or even cared about. I didn't need friends and definitely not friends like that. I'd already learned that lesson in high school. I didn't even answer phone calls from anyone in my life anymore. I only cared really about soothing my pain. Selfish asshole that I was.

"You don't care about me. You don't care about the kids. You only care about yourself."

"What the fuck is that supposed to mean, Joyce? I work all day, every day to support this family."

"You're never home. I have to be around them all the time. They don't like me."

Dad started laughing. "What do you mean they don't like you? What a stupid excuse for me to come home."

"Oh, I didn't realise you needed an excuse to come home. None of it matters to you anymore, does it? This life we've built. I need your help with Rory. I can't be alone with him."

"Come on Joyce. You have to find a way."

I hear a glass shatter. "You promised we were in this together."

My dad whispered to my mom, "You have to try, sweetie. He deserves it."

Her sobs curdled in her throat and in my ears. I was ten years old, and old enough to understand my mom didn't love me, and old enough to understand there wasn't anything I could do about it.

My dad walked past me on his way out of the conversation and stopped with me at his feet. I looked up at him, my tower of a father, and thought *oh I'm in trouble now*. He just looked down at me and smiled, the same way he used to when he asked me to help him peel potatoes in the kitchen, and said "I love you, Rory."

With years tacked onto my life I learned that smile came from a place of discomfort and obligation, trying to cover up what couldn't be unsaid. The closeness we shared was all forced, and though he knew now what I'd heard, we rarely talked about it.

I stood outside of the Humanities building and sucked the end of my cigarette, watching people go by sharing private jokes and subtle intimacies. I imagined my life like theirs, wishing I had it in me to flow so easily with others. Though I wanted and needed someone, I needed a drink more. I spat on the ground, disgusted at my unquenchable self-indulgence.

Chapter Twelve

It was mid-afternoon and the leaves were falling from the trees like they'd been choreographed. I watched them flit onto the ground and felt myself wrapped in a daze of longing and fortitude. I searched through the restored contacts in my new phone and dialled impulsively.

"I need you, like bad. Real bad." Unaware how upset I was until I heard myself speak.

"Who is this?" Ellie asked. As soon as I heard her voice I felt I'd made a mistake.

I cleared my throat, willed myself to sound saner. "It's Rory."

"Rory Langford?"

"Yeah." My tongue went dry at the sound of her uneasiness.

"Why are you calling me? I can't talk right now. I'm sorry."

"Wait..." I hadn't meant to yell. There was a

silence between us as I tried to catch my breath. "My dad died. Can we meet for coffee today?"

I heard her sigh. "I'm sorry to hear about your dad, I really am. But I can't see you. I'm sorry."

"Please, please. I need you. I need to see you. Please."

"Rory, I'm not doing this with you. I haven't heard from you in five years. This is not okay. I can't see you, I'm sorry."

"Please, I'm scared of myself. I don't trust myself. I don't trust anyone. I keep thinking that I'm gonna get better. Every day I wake up and it's worse Ell, it's so fucking bad I can't even look at myself. I just need to see someone, anyone who knows me. I just need to not feel so alone. I don't have any friends. I don't have anyone. Please, Ellie, please." There was a silence on the other end. I thought maybe she had hung up, I half hoped that she had.

"Why did you choose to call me? Where's Jordan? Your sister?"

"Don't talk to me about them. Please don't talk to me about all the things I've fucked up. I know I fucked up. I just really want to end it all right now, I have nothing. Nothing to lose, nothing to gain. I'm scared of myself. I don't know who I am anymore."

"Okay, okay, calm down. Where are you? I can meet you in an hour. We can go for coffee."

"Thank you, thank you so much." I started to cry.

"Yeah, just text me the place, I'll see you in a

bit. Bye." She hung up before I could respond. I understood why she was so reluctant to meet me, but if anyone knew what I sounded like when I was at my most desperate, it was her. She was there through it all, through what I thought had been my worst.

I went straight to the coffee shop. It was only three blocks from my house, so I could wait there and see her walk in. I hated being late, the awkward way my feet moved. I had drunk three glasses of rye before leaving the house so I thought I'd better order a coffee to mask the smell. The guy at the counter looked at me like he thought I was revolting, pasted his customer service smile on and asked me what I wanted. "Need a chaser?"

"What?"

He looked irritated, the way people do when their dumb jokes don't land.

"You smell awful."

"Huh. I thought that was you."

He handed me a cup of coffee. "I didn't order this."

"You need it though, don't you?"

I walked away with the coffee, charmed by the shitty customer service, and drank it knowing that it didn't mix well with the anxiety I was feeling about seeing Ellie again.

I watched her pull up in front of the door, park and sit in her car for fifteen minutes. As my anxiety built I considered making moves to go out and meet her, but I was frozen to my chair, sipping coffee I didn't want. When she eventually walked through the door I didn't know whether or not to stand up so I looked down at the ground. She sat next to me and looked into my face. I almost cried at the sight of her. She looked like home. Time had really done good with her. She didn't smile or make any warm gesture or movement.

"Hey stranger." As soon as I said this I regretted it. She got up to get a coffee and I was still kicking myself when she got back.

"How are you holding up?" she asked me, though I could tell she already knew the answer.

"Not."

She just nodded, looked around the room, fidgeted with her keys on the table.

"I'm in school now."

"Wow, crazy."

"Yeah, crazy." I couldn't even make eye contact with her. Couldn't even think of anything to say. I was so afraid that she would leave if I didn't say something so I started talking.

"You're the only person who really knows me. I'm losing it like everyone always thought I would. My fucking dad, I miss him."

"I know how much he meant to you." She said to her hands. People don't know what to say when someone dies. They want you to keep talking or to stop talking or whatever option takes away the pressure for them to formulate a reasonable response, even though there isn't one.

"Yeah, I'm sorry for calling you."

"It's okay."

"I really loved you, you know." I immediately took a sip from my empty coffee cup, unsure why I said this. Stupid mouth fucking me over again. She looked uncomfortable. She gave me a thin smile, drank her coffee and fixed her eyes on something on the other side of the room.

"What's new with you?" I tried to redeem myself with small talk.

"Nothing really, got a job in accounting, really boring but pays well."

"Well that's good."

"Yeah. So what are you taking in school?"

"Philosophy."

"That's very you of you." She was just trying to be nice, there was nothing genuine in her voice. I never should have bothered her in her life after she had moved on from me. I was a disastrous person to try to love back then and the longer I looked at her face, the more it became clear to me that we didn't know each other anymore, that she had just come here out of that deep sense of pity I had always evoked in her.

"So, what exactly do you want from me?" she asked.

"Nothing."

"Hmm." She turned to look at me. "Are you still

drinking?" She said it softly like it was a shameful secret.

"Sometimes."

She nodded slowly at me, knowing that moderation for me was an impossible feat.

"Do you think we could ever, go for dinner or something? I just want to know you again." My dumb drunk mouth was getting way further ahead of me than I'd planned. "I always regret not having done better with you than I did. I still think about you a lot. I still miss you, a lot."

She closed her eyes. "Rory, it's been years since we've seen each other. You know that I always will care about you, but things have changed for me. I can't just go running back to my past, I don't want that for myself."

"I don't want that for you either. But I'm different now. I'm not the same person that I was back then."

"You absolutely reek of alcohol right now." She made no effort to keep her voice down this time.

"No. I don't. I just. Yeah, I had a few, I don't know. I miss my dad." I rambled, rubbing my sweaty hand across my pants. "I just wanted to be next to you again."

"You're drunk. I told you before that I couldn't deal with this. I'm not doing this with you now. I've come a long way since back then."

"Then why are you here?"

"Because you called me frantically. You were

scaring me. Because I know how you are when things get bad. Please don't read too much into it. I didn't mean to give you the wrong idea. I just wanted to make sure that you were okay." She wasn't budging her expression at all, her emotions were completely level in comparison to mine. She did know me better than anyone after all.

"Can we go somewhere else?" I could feel people staring, out of the corners of their eyes while engaged in conversations with other people. Everything was a show. I couldn't stomach it.

"No. I came here for coffee with you but I can't stay, okay?"

"Why not?"

She had always been the sweetest person that anyone could know. She would talk someone through a bad day even if she hated them. In fact I don't think she actually hated anyone. She wanted the best for everyone. I don't know how she remained so calm all the time, so assertive in expressing what she needed, but it inspired me. I wanted to be a better person, be more like she was.

"I can't be with you. I care about you but I think you need to find other friends to talk to. I just don't have those feelings for you anymore. I'm not stuck in the past like that, I've moved on. You should move on too. I really want you to be happy."

"It's not like I didn't have a good reason to call you."

"Maybe you did, but I can't be with someone

who is so in love with destroying himself that he doesn't even have time to like me."

"I'm different now. I told you that." I was getting angry.

"I have a career now, a long-term boyfriend. I have stuff going on in my life and you and I, we're in the past. I wanted to make sure you were okay. I wanted to make sure that you weren't going to hurt yourself but that's all I can do. I can't be the one that's here for you this time. I'm sorry but I'm not going to change my mind. You need to find what you're really searching for, because it isn't me."

I should have known she came here out of guilt, nothing else, just some sense of obligation, some selfish need to not have my blood on her hands. I couldn't even hate her for that because I wanted so badly to love someone.

"I really, really hope that you get the help you need." As soon as she finished her coffee she was putting her coat on to leave.

"Wait, please don't go."

"I have to get home. I'm sorry." She stood up, so I did too.

"No, wait. I'm sorry I made you uncomfortable, can we just start over? Please?"

She looked at me with so much pity it forced the blood out of my face. "People who have been where we have together can't start over. I have to go. I really hope that you'll be okay." Just as soon as she was out of the coffee shop I forgot what it felt like to want her so desperately.

She was uncomfortable around me. Even the people who had once fallen into the patterns of my life with such ease were uncomfortable around me now.

I expected this rejection, maybe it had even been the whole reason I called her, but still I was left with a sense of loss like I was seventeen and losing her all over again. I wished I could have kept my tongue under control long enough to tell her what I actually wanted to say instead of letting myself come off as a drunk, desperate lunatic pining over his ex.

I barely even thought about her, except when I felt most vulnerable to all the mistakes I had made with my sorry excuse for a life. The impulse to call her only came from a deep need for me to remind myself of times when I was less out of control, times when I still could have walked myself out of it if I wanted to. Times when there were still people there who could tolerate being near me. I felt like a child sitting in that coffee shop without her, staring at the door she had left through like I could reverse time and make her come back to me.

Chapter Thirteen

"We're closing. Time to leave."

The thing I liked most about dingy, dark university bars at night was the lack of customer service from the staff. I didn't like to be talked to, waited on, asked if I was okay. I've always been a shit liar.

Working my throat muscles to keep the whisky down. Booze has been making me sick but I can't let that stop me. I wave to the bartender on my way out, who looks at me out of the corner of his eye and avoids full acknowledgment.

I come here infrequently, when other bars seem too far away, or when I can't wait the distance home to have a drink. I make people uncomfortable by proximity because I don't know how to sit, what to look at, at what angle my smile is supposed to fit on my face. I'm often met with down gazes and quick excuses to be left alone.

Empty flask, empty stomach, empty echoing head. What else could really get me out the door of my own shitty life to a party, where people interact with you, where the weight of social obligation and societal norms presses down on your lungs with pot smoke and other people's musk? I found other people irritating for the most part, so I tried my best to avoid them. It always left me with this sickening feeling, like no matter how hard I tried I just wouldn't be able to do it right. I wouldn't be able to say the right words to fit in with whoever was standing in front of me, like they'd somehow sense what I really was.

You can't really walk up to the doors of a frat house and not think of it as some method of self-harm. There has to be at least an ounce of self-loathing in you to bring you to a place like this. The piss-coloured shit house was on my way home and I wasn't drunk enough to put myself to bed yet. I could feel the regret before I even walked up to the door. I wanted to breach the parameters I'd set for myself. Hurt myself badly, watch someone reflect my self-hatred and put me in my place in the dirt. I was always told that I needed to socialise more, try to have friends and hold down some sort of healthy life that involved numerous other people. I just couldn't bring myself to do that. It felt like too much. I could hardly keep up with the banter that I shared with only me in my own head.

"Hey Toby!" Some basketball of a man flung himself at another man.

"Get off me you faggot." Toby replied.

I watched the muscles flying lifeless from the arrogant bodies they were attached to. People living to impress faces that wouldn't remember them five months after meeting. Taking commemorative pictures to document the parties they would brag about having been to, hosted, and puked at, when their desk jobs aged them too young and they needed to convince themselves and others that they had once, in fact, been partially alive.

I looked for Andy, my needless anger boiling somewhere under my sternum. I clenched my fists against the pain I was so desperate to feel. I headed for the keg. I wasn't much of a beer drinker really, only drank it when I was trying to remain in control, but any booze was good booze in a place like this. There were a bunch of bros hanging around the keg, looking for a reason to fight anyone. I was elated to finally be in a place where nothing would save me, where the very look of me was provocation enough.

"Hey bro, what are you after?" A big, tall, lanky looking motherfucker put his arm around me.

"I just want a cup of beer, could you keep your fucking hands off me?"

"Ooh, that's what all the ladies always say. And you know what I say back?"

His friends started laughing, two of them high-fived each other.

"I say no. Two nos make a yes buddy, if you know what I'm saying."

"What the fuck did you just say?" My mouth said, followed by an ear-splitting silence. One laugh came from some asshole's face.

"We've got ourselves a sissy here, boys." He was standing unreasonably close to my face. My heart was pumping too much blood into my body for me to keep upright. I reached out to hold the table next to me, dizzying and feeling woozy.

"Forget what I just said, it's all good man." I closed my eyes to make the room stop spinning.

"Oh, he wants me to forget what he said. You know, it doesn't work that way around here. You come in here and try to talk tough to me, I'm gonna make sure you see that shit through." He finished his beer and crushed the can on his head.

I looked on at all the guys watching, standing back a way, trying to look smug. The thing is, I could see through it all, my eyes x-raying their fear. None of them had an ounce of anything but cowardice in them. That's the only reason people really lord themselves around in places like these anyways. They don't trust their baseline identity enough, they have to chase after something that resembles control. If only they all knew control was an illusion, it would scare the shit out of them.

I braced myself for the skinny little shits to try

and take me down, but instead the next thing I knew I was being lifted into the air by my legs, tipped upside down with a nozzle shoved in my mouth. As if a keg stand was a punishment. After a few seconds it really did start to feel like one. I could hardly hear the people chanting around me, their voices came through my ears as though we were all under water. Beer was leaking down my face and my body was trembling. Couldn't breathe.

I fell to the floor when they let go of me and traced my pulse with my fingers, trying to shush it and calm myself down.

"You good, bro?" he asked as he kicked me in the ribs. I heard myself groan and forced myself to stand up, bits of vomit flying from my lips. My footsteps slurred as I began moving away from the crowd. I had to get out of this hell hole. I knew from the get-go I was walking into a place full of the people I hated most, but there's something different about really experiencing it.

I stood for a minute in the middle of the living room. People's footsteps, shouts, and laughter blurring and swimming through my eyes and ears. The room spun with all the things I could never be, my eyes were puking madly again and I didn't want to be crying at a frat house in front of all these human shit bricks. I was frozen in a timeframe of utter loss for myself, for what moulds I never would fit into, my skin tightening and loosening with the beating of my heart.

"Hey man, the fuck's the matter with you?" A guy laughed in my ear. I clenched a fist and turned to meet him.

"Yo, it's cool, it's cool. You just seem kinda, not alright you know?"

"Yeah, well not everything is all good all the time so just fuck off." I said.

"Defensive much? You need a water?"

"I need a fucking IV."

"Amen to that."

He had tired eyes, and a really isolated face. He stepped into my space and we both stood there for hundreds of years, watching the shit around us.

"I'm Blake."

"Rory."

"Good to meet you, Rory. You go to school here?"

"Yeah, I mean sorta."

"Sorta?" He laughed.

"I don't really go, I'm just kinda enrolled but I don't really give a fuck."

"Why not?"

"Do you really give a fuck? I mean, really give a fuck?" I asked.

"Does anyone?"

"Oh yeah man, some people completely lose their whole soul in this elitist shit. I mean look at where we are."

"Yeah. I guess. You into music?"

"Who isn't into music?"

"A lot of people who say they are. Anyway, my band is playing a show next weekend, you should stop by."

"When?"

"Here, I'll put my number in your phone. Text me and I'll send you the deetz, get you on the guest list."

Somewhat reluctantly, I handed him my phone. He put his number in, handed it back and smiled.

"You want a drink?" I asked.

"I actually don't drink. But I should get out of here, I'll see you around." He was already walking away from me before I could respond.

Who the fuck comes to a frat party and doesn't drink? Or was he just trying to make me feel bad? Walking around a room full of fuck-ups with his sobriety, mocking them. Fucking dick. Pretentious asshole.

On my way out the door I saw a two-six of whisky sitting on a table with a bunch of other neighbouring bottles of lesser alcohols. No one was paying attention to me so I grabbed it. I laughed in the general direction of all the shit and walked out the door. Once on the front lawn I finally found Andy. His smug face beamed at my arrival.

"Hey buddy, you made–" I stopped his speech with my fist. I took a swig of whisky, the whole world simmering around me, my ears ringing somewhere in the distance. Someone behind me told me I shouldn't have done that. Another person screamed. Someone's throat closed against the pressure of a fist, I guess it must have been mine.

What a great feat. To aggravate these slabs of ham. If I were more of a man, less of a masochist, I might have tried to stop them, defend myself, care a little. I felt my body break the surface of a wall, a crack of plaster or bone I wasn't sure. Andy was pouring a drink into my mouth. I jammed my throat shut and spat it back in his face. These fuckers were really trying to kill me with alcohol. I guess I could relate. The whisky bottle in my hand shattered at my feet, I prayed that it would soak into my ankles and make its way into my bloodstream.

I felt hands, heard someone's scream from a mile away. Someone yelling stop or don't or please and it could have been me but I left the pains of regular living behind and was riding the trance of blackness, compounding myself before any fists had altered me. Three or maybe five, could have been two guys dragged me into the alleyway behind the house and thought they were winning while giving me exactly what I'd come for.

I hope this initiation was enough for Andy to succeed at being a scum-sucking bottom feeder with the rest of these goons. The last sound I heard myself make was a wild laugh mixed with a scream. The adrenaline pumping through me could only make me numb and I hoped like hell I would never wake up to my life again.

Chapter Fourteen

Drills in my head. Hospital life tanks and life bags and piss bags dropped at my feet. Nurses rushing around my head barely seeable, and I am the size of a pea to them. Checking clipboards for my name.

"Rory Langford? You have a call from your dad."

"No thanks."

Nurses arguing in the hall over this:

"Well, he's over the age of eighteen."

"It's his dad."

"He's legally allowed to refuse."

"We can't discharge him without someone to pick him up."

"Maybe there's someone else?"

"It's best if it's a family member."

"Some people's families are no good. Who knows what we could be releasing him to? Ask him who he'd like to call or we can extend his seventy-two-hour hold."

"We need the bed for new patients."

Asking favours of people wasn't my strong suit but it got easier the less of me was left over. The nurse briefly explained to me that I had slit my wrists and taken a lot of pills, as if I didn't already know that. I didn't make eye contact with her the entire time because I was too annoyed at still being alive. They whispered about me as though I couldn't hear them. I became less of a person.

Jordan came as quick as the call had been made, like he had been waiting for it. In a way I think most of the people in my life had been waiting for it. I was shovelled out of the bed like a corpse, minus the benefit of being one. They got my name wrong a number of times. As if being treated like a subhuman would make me any happier to be alive.

"You're lucky you survived this." She smiled at me, as though she couldn't imagine a reality where someone might not feel lucky to be alive. As if trying to kill yourself was always a mistake, and any person waking up after the fact would be met with a grand transcendent joy to be given another chance instead of a desperate need to try again as soon as the sliding doors closed behind them.

I couldn't try again with Jordan there. He always brought humour with him by the bucketful. If you weren't laughing with Jordan you were with somebody else.

I never had to explain alienation to Jordan. He was rushed from foster home to foster home.

Alienation lived under his heart and was the driving force behind everything he did.

Jordan kept track of me when I lost track of myself. He'd seen people go down a similar road to the one I was currently on. Why he kept me around when I was only making the same mistakes that he'd already tried to reconcile in other people is beyond me. I never hated him, even when he was calling me out in one of his unbroken monologues:

"Some people think they can spend their whole lives running, running, running. If you're running from yourself, you're gonna fuck yourself over, Rory. You can't do that shit. There's always going to be someone who'll tell you to just get over it, but I know how stubborn that goddamn disease is. People are like, hey let's go for drinks, hey let's do blow, hey lets fuck ourselves up. But then, where are they when you start getting a little too fucked up, and it's not fun anymore? What happens when there's nowhere left to run?"

I remember promising myself I'd never be just another drunk in Jordan's life. Even though I'd broken that promise to myself again and again, he never got fed up with me about it. He had a way of making you forget you were miserable, if only for a moment.

We balanced each other out in a lot of ways and he was capable of things I could only dream of. Jordan was so confident with everyone that it made me uncomfortable. I watched the way he acted around other people, like he was truly alright with himself. He never treated anyone unkindly.

I think there are many types of people, but if Jordan and I were divided into just two categories, he'd be in the one where he's lost everything and because of it, he knows he can survive. He knows how to deal with the aftermath. Then there's me. I've lost everything and don't even have a firm grasp on what kind of person I am, so I have absolutely no interest in losing more, or finding out what it feels like to lose more.

Jordan was the only person I ever talked to about what really hurt me. It made me feel drunk to talk about it. I didn't have to put a single ounce of liquor between my lips when I decided to open up, I could instantly feel my body floating away, but I never liked that kind of drunk.

When Jordan picked me up from the hospital, it was instant laughter. He made me feel like I hadn't tried to kill myself, and he never asked how I was doing or what was going on, or what was wrong with me, because he already knew.

"Wanna pick up some babes? They love a sad pathetic shit like you."

"Very funny. I have a headache."

"You wanna stay with me a bit? We can plot out a revolution or something relaxing like that."

"Yeah, that would be good."

"Your wish is God's command."

Jordan made a lot of jokes about religion. The foster family that ended up adopting him was intensely religious. The kinds of dogmatic people who don't let you say hell, even though they're so drunk they can't see straight. I found this out the hard way when I went over for dinner one time and said that organised religion was a load of dogshit. Jordan thought it was hilarious but his foster father never liked me after that.

Jordan snuck out of his house all the time and would bring me these weird folk punk mixes with Pat the Bunny on them.

Once Jordan escaped from the constraints of his upbringing and his neo religious foster family, he let me stay with him all the time. He got a dingy apartment, decorated it with photos of Karl Marx despite not believing in communism whatsoever and wrote things that inspired him on the photographs from time to time. If you asked him why Karl Marx, he'd say something like, "I dunno, the dude had a lot to say. I've got a lot to say. Plus I like his beard."

Not a day with Jordan went by where I didn't learn some strange thing about the world. He had something to say about everything and never expected anyone to agree with him, didn't care. He always told me that his manifesto came out his ass every morning and he couldn't keep up to write it down.

The best memory I have of Jordan, and one I could never repay him for, is the time he took me for a long drive after I told him the truth about my family. He talked to me all night long, and I listened, absorbed it, and then lost his consolation somewhere inside of me. Even when I went back to my painfully shitty way of being, after promising him I would try to change for the better, he still accepted me with an unconditionality that only he has.

I knew better than to think that him picking me up at the hospital was going to work out. This time I went too far. He tried to act natural at first, but he couldn't keep it up. He cracked one joke and then there was silence the rest of the time. Maybe Jordan only pretends not to be afraid of losing things.

"Jordan, I'm sorry."

"Hell man, people love you, ya know? You may be a sorry sucker to be around, but people love you."

We drove in silence.

"I know that, but it hurts, it hurts a lot."

"Yeah, fuck it, let's not go there today, alright?"

He was tired of me, and after this last favor I knew I couldn't stay. I humoured him for a few weeks, and I went to work as was promised in my treatment plan: I would stay on track in my life, try to win myself back. I saved all the money I was making and got a new apartment. I didn't tell Jordan any of this because I didn't want him keeping an eye on me anymore.

The days we spent together after my release from the hospital left me feeling emptier and emptier. He watched me in the same way my sister did, with this apprehension that was all-encompassing. He tried to hide it the way my mother tried to hide that she didn't love me, with absolutely no success. And yeah, we had fun at one time, but I knew now that it would never be the same again.

I left pieces of myself in heaps next to so many people's sofas because I was embarrassed about moving on. I didn't like endings so I tried to create clean transitions, ones where I could avoid confronting departure so nothing ever felt truly over.

I knew Jordan wouldn't be my friend after disappearing and ignoring all his phone calls but what did I care? He wanted to stop me from doing what I wanted to do. He wanted to stop me from feeling what I felt, protect me from it as though I didn't have a right to destroy myself.

Some babies hang themselves with their mothers' umbilical cords and I wonder often if that would have made my mom happier or sadder. All I could really think about when I was with Jordan was how I wished I could laugh like him, how I wanted so badly to break free from it all like he had, but when he looked at me, I knew that he hadn't fully gotten out and that's why I had to leave. I wasn't going to bring down another person I loved.

I didn't forgive myself for the way he looked at me when I was in the hospital. Or rather, the way he didn't really look at me.

And all this is because I couldn't kill myself properly. I couldn't remove myself from my family properly. Now I just needed to be alone to clean up my life.

Jordan and I wouldn't see each other again, that was something I knew because when I decided someone wasn't a part of my life anymore, I tried not to go back on it. I didn't think in absolutes unless it came to abandonment. He started to remind me of every mistake I was making and I needed to live apart from that reminder.

He left messages on my voicemail for weeks afterwards. I had finally made Jordan angry. Jordan had never been an angry dude before he met me but I frustrated him to the core and I knew it.

He said I should have at least left a note, said goodbye. What killed me most was when he said that I was the one person he had ever known that he felt sure would never abandon him, and now he wasn't sure anymore if anyone was reliable.

Chapter Fifteen

I woke up the next day to my brain being fucked with a razor blade. Maybe the whisky had finally killed me this time. I could sense the presence of other human beings and it annoyed me before I even saw who they were. I hardly remembered the events from the night before. I must have been lucid at certain times because there are visuals that stick out to me in memory now. But at the time I couldn't tell them apart from dream or reality.

I opened my eyes as much as I could, and the pounding in my head worsened. I forced myself to sit up, slump against the wall I had been sleeping next to. I could hardly move. One or more of my bones felt fractured or broken. I had a headache from my eyeballs to my asshole. Radiation of physical memories from the night before. Either being dead felt worse than being alive or I had lived through it. My bandages were tattered around the edges, leaving some of my stitches exposed, torn, blood smeared all over my arm. I could move my eyes in my head just enough to soak in some of my surroundings. The clinging cigarette stench wasn't helping the blood clotting in my nose. The walls were yellow, the floors were carpeted in dust. The place looked unleasable, unliveable, and yet more pleasant than the inside of my head. I pulled a dirty condom off my skin and flinched only as much as my body would allow me to move. I looked up again and saw the rusted end of a switchblade inches away from my face.

"I know what you're thinking. Don't fucking try anything. I will kill you. I don't give a fuck."

"Okay. Hey, do you have a cigarette?"

She handed me one without taking her eyes from me or moving the knife from my face.

"Lighter?" I leaned down to light my cigarette and exhaled, keeping my eyes on the blade, grateful for its presence between us.

"Don't fucking move."

"Couldn't if I wanted to." I laid back down on the floor and she stared at me with wild eyes, keeping the knife steady in her hand.

"I will cut your fucking fingers off if you touch me."

I just looked at her, bored and annoyed. "Okay, so who the fuck are you?"

"Yeah, like you don't know."

"I actually don't."

She lowered the knife at my indifference. "My name's Natalie. You were beat up pretty bad last night. Thought I'd fix you up. But don't get any ideas." The knife again.

I was already tired of this. As if I needed any more drama. "Put the knife down. I'm not going to hurt you."

She stared at me and started to cry. The sound was uncomfortable and made my head hurt worse. The smells and the sounds of the room. The dry skin caked on her face. The screeching of her voice. "Dude, please. I have a fucking headache."

"Yeah, everyone has a fucking headache don't they?" She got up and fell back on the ground, crying harder, like a toddler. "Get the fuck away from me, okay? I helped you, now leave." She screamed this last bit. If I could've moved, I would've left her to her neurotic meltdown but my body was too swollen and I just wanted to enjoy a cigarette, so I watched her mutter to herself and cry herself calm. It didn't take long for her mood to switch. She crawled back over to me and sighed a long, raspy breath that made her cough. "Can I talk to you about something?"

"Uh, I guess so."

"Never mind, you don't care." She looked away from me, wanting me to argue this.

"Well, not really to be honest." I butted my cigarette out on the floor.

"Hey, you can't put that out there, you fucking asshole."

I looked at all the cigarette butts keeping mine company. "Okay." I picked it up and put it in my pocket.

"That's gonna make your clothes smell like shit, dude."

I closed my eyes and took a long breath. "Alright, what would you like me to do with it then?"

She held out her hand. I put the cigarette butt in it and she put it in her pocket. Some people just don't make any fucking sense.

"So, can I talk to you about something?"

"Sure. Whatever. I don't give a shit." My legs were throbbing. I was afraid to stand on them. My head hurt so bad I could hardly feel the rest of my body.

"You know, when I was a kid, my dad wasn't a drunk, but he was angry. So fucking angry. The way he hit my mom. He would just hit her, you know?" She paused and she bit her lip. She sucked on it for a little while. "I was only six the first time I saw it."

Why the fuck did people keep coming to me with their fucked-up stories? But hearing her talk somehow made my body hurt less. I was transfixed by her in one part of my chest and in the other I felt a queasiness beyond any sense of dread that left me longing and desperate to rip my skin off, head first. She talked and talked, words that hardly made it through me, words I didn't want to hear or care about. All I could do was nod and then:

"Um, thanks for helping me last night but I really should get going." I realised I had been holding my breath, trying not to vomit up my whole heart waiting for her to stop talking. The story of her life seeped through me in bits, where I shifted from annoyance to compassion all too quickly.

Her mom, her dad, her shitty boyfriend. The betrayals that she woke up to everyday. The life she had been forced into. She had her eyes fixed on a spot a few inches from my face, moving her mouth with the pace of her warped childhood memories. She talked slowly to me, pushing each word through the fog in my head, ignoring my plea for escape.

"I'm sorry. I just I hate it, I fucking hate it. It's all garbage bullshit." She took a deep breath. She grabbed my knee, held onto it so tight I thought it would pop out of its socket.

"I'm sorry, fuck. You're just an innocent guy. I misjudged you, okay? I haven't talked to anyone for so long. Max won't listen to me. God forbid anyone has a problem aside from him. That stupid fat fuck. I hate him."

I nodded again.

"What the hell happened to you anyway? Your face is really fucked up, man."

"Frat party."

"Ah, fuck."

"Look, I just really wanna rest." I tried to say this in a way that was calm and collected but it came out as aggravated, the way it felt inside of me to begin with I guess. I couldn't listen to her anymore; I couldn't make any space for it.

"Yeah, whatever. Fucking rest then. See if I care. I just wanted to tell you that Max is not abusive and I don't care what anyone says."

"I don't even know who Max is. I don't even know who you are."

"Yeah you say that like it's a bad thing. What I wouldn't give to not know me. Fuck off then. I just wanted a break."

I made to stand up and look around, check if my legs still worked. They didn't, so I sat back down. We looked at each other for what felt like twelve murky years. I forced myself to want to hear what she had to say. Surrender to being so alive I couldn't stand it anymore, so alive I'd burst through and maybe start living for real.

She told me about what she'd left, what parts stayed and what she'd never been able to wash off. It was hard sitting in my body while she spoke. She had a self-awareness I'd never known, yet hardly aware of what her reality was, or how similar it was to the things she was telling me about that she swore were in the past. But you get used to things, even if that means you're inhaling dust and calling it breathing.

Her monologue lived in my head. I lost pieces of it as quickly as they came. I watched her father beat her. I watched her boyfriend threaten her. I watched the cowardly, slimey way he slinked around the room. I watched her taunted and torn apart. I couldn't feel my heart beating anymore. I couldn't open my mouth to speak. My tongue was glued to the roof of it. In between her words I tried to remember how I got here. It scared me that I couldn't. I wondered what else I had lost in that particular chunk of blackness.

She talked until she fell asleep on the floor. I put a blanket over her that smelled like mildew, but I knew she wouldn't mind, which made me really sad. I tucked her hair behind her ear, grabbed my stuff, took out twenty dollars, put it in her pocket and left. I was relieved that the ranting was finally over, but grieving the dissonance all the same.

As soon as I'd used all my energy standing up, I was kicked back to the ground. I looked up at a coked out guy with greasy hair and clothes that could have fit him five years prior.

"Who the fuck are you?" I coughed out of the body that no longer felt like mine.

"I'm Max, who the fuck are you? Did you fuck her?" He kicked me again. I was annoyed at this— how many people were going to kick me before I could finally go home and have a drink? He turned on Natalie, started shaking her, yelling "Did you fuck him you dirty whore? Did you fuck him?" He lifted me against the wall and spat in my face "I better not see you again, I'll fucking kill you."

Natalie jumped up to intervene. Max smacked her across the face. She started crying from a place only the most haunted people have in them to cry from. "He didn't fuck me, Max." She sobbed.

"You're a fucking whore." He had her around the neck, shoved her to the ground and turned back to me. "Get the fuck out of here, doesn't look like it'd take much to finish you off. And I fucking will. I'll fucking kill you."

My cracked throat, "Get off her." I stood up, limping over to him.

"Mind your own fucking business. This is between me and my bitch." He kneed me again in the stomach. My vision went black, mouth filled with blood. My body forced me to exit the situation. It started moving against any thought. I managed to drag the pathetic thing out the door, slink down the stairs. I fought my head for leaving, but all the same I tried to forget the mercy Natalie's words had submitted me to. The fractured bones I was whining about were nothing more than blemishes and bruises compared to what she had to live with. I'd been fucked hard by feet bigger and more privileged than mine but never had lived through anything like she had.

I heard her screaming all the way out the door. I hated myself for being too weak to fight. I hated myself for being hurt the way I was. For my folding ribs and bleeding mouth. I hated the swelling in my head. I was reluctant to leave, but one more swift knee to the abdomen left me crawling back to my life.

I turned back once to look at Max through the glint of pain in my eyes, entering the space she occupied, cutting through my blurred vision and disappearing where no one could protect her.

Chapter Sixteen

When you're six years old and you hear your mom's back against the sink, unsure if the cracking sound is the porcelain or her bones, unsure which is more delicate, you don't ever forget that. It's not as though you know anything about how the world is supposed to interact. It's confusing to hear your friends talk about their parents: the trips to Disneyland, the laughter over pot roast and soccer games. The tiny tales of love that meet you in the playground and sound nothing like the inside of your house. It's not as though you know what love is supposed to look like, if it's supposed to be broken windows and empty cupboards. If love is supposed to be cold bed sheets and neglect.

Waiting at the top of the stairs for your dad to stop yelling at your mom so you can ask her for help with your homework. The pages wrinkling under your fingers, paper sticking to your sweating palms. You hear words you know nothing about except that you shouldn't repeat them, and you only know this because of the weight they seem to carry. Once you figure out later in life what these words mean they will crawl under your skin like parasites and eat your flesh until you're cold and lonely and made of bone. How are you supposed to know that the sound of shattering glass, breaking plaster, and renditions of "fuck you, psycho cunt" will always sound like some cryptic "I love you" for the rest of your life?

It's not as though you have any place else to go. When you're six years old, you're forced to experience this. And it's too early in life to understand that daddy is a bad person. You love him the way only a six-year-old heart knows how to love, when sorry is enough to justify still loving him. When your heart never ages past six years old and sorry forever becomes enough to reconcile the crimes others commit on your body. It's not as though you know what he's capable of, or how sorry is smaller than you are now, and weighs a hell of a lot less than you do.

But as your mom says, you don't know anything about love yet. You're too young to understand how complicated the relationships are between two adults. What you do know is that your house is scary. You know that it's more haunted than any old abandoned house that the neighbourhood kids run past on their way home. It's scarier than burning yourself on a hot frying pan trying to move out of dad's way when he's in a hurry. You know that nothing is scarier than walking through the doors of what should be your sanctuary and hearing the people you love most in the world who are supposed to protect you, beating and being beaten. You know that your house is haunted with ghosts most people couldn't imagine, and it's not as if you can do anything about it but grow addicted to the chaos, create it everywhere you go for fear of silence and the unpredictability that comes with it. Knowing if the storm isn't occurring now, then it must be on its way.

Chapter Seventeen

Self-loathing is the driving force that keeps me alive. Under that, there isn't much else to me. That's what I tell myself, so I can justify my mother.

Only one of my radio speakers works in my car, and the cold air leaks in now because of the cracked glass on my back window. It stings my face and I love the way it feels, like someone is pouring Listerine on my wounds. Nothing hurts anymore because of the images stuck in my head. All I can see is Natalie, what abstract memory I have of her. Her face shifts and blurs in that studio in my head where I keep her. I can sense the room, the dust, the smoke, my father hitting my mother. Johnny B. Goode is on the radio and I know I shouldn't be driving because my legs keep seizing up when I try to hit the brakes and I putt along at red lights, nearly getting hit each time I try to stop. I can only put one hand on the steering wheel because my other one is bleeding and swollen. The hand that works isn't my dominant one and there are so many cuts on my legs, they reopen every time I step on the gas. It keeps me awake. I don't know if being unconscious counts as sleep, but if it does, I sure am well rested.

The nausea takes hold of me every so often, and I have to fight against it to stay upright. I feel puke rise onto my tongue. I swallow it. devote myself to the road and the act of going forward. The pain is like knives in my gut. I wish it would come out my asshole, but it never seems to. I'm used to it most days. It's dull and persistent and has stuck with me the past seven years. It begs my attention periodically, but I hate doctors and I hate eating so my stomach will have to fuck off and take a hint.

I was having a bit of a panic and I talked out loud to Jordan in my car: "I'm doing it, Jordan. I'm taking the eternal and holding it in my gut all the way to my mother. I'm giving back her birth of me through an ethereal and weird expression of desperation. And I'm hoping for the best." And I imagined him talking back to me: "Rory, this might not go well." Because he would always prepare me for that, and my naivety would play with me and say: "I can survive the things that don't go well." And he would say back: "Is this what you call surviving? It doesn't look like you're doing much of that these days." And I knew he was right. But I would argue with him and say: "There are breaths in my lungs. Even if they're short, they are there. And my legs are bending by extension of my brain processing the material of my external reality at an acceptable speed. And my eyes blink once every few seconds to prevent my eyes from drying out so that I can focus on what I perceive to be real. And my heart is beating a bit out of order, but see? It's still there in its cavity, working for me." And Jordan would say: "Rory, you're shaking, burning calories just with the exhausting act of staying alive." And I would say: "Who said I was alive? I don't think I feel that way. I just am something though, some strangeness that moves through some strangeness and comes out the other side recognised or ignored." And Jordan would say: "That's fucking absurd. Give it to Marx." And then I could feel a pen in my fingertips and I had to pull over to write some things down.

The tail end of my car was inserted unwisely close to the road, and people honked at me as I frantically extracted the words that shook through my wrong hand.

If time is well spent in the before and after, what is the during? The present moment doesn't really have much, and boredom makes people sick. Only because in boredom, restlessness, there becomes an existential dread that makes hair stand on end. Then we are really left looking at the strange unseeable substance that rests somewhere on or in our bodies, which are so weird to have. If you think about the fingertips too much you lose them, they become a question in a void of questions that all patter around each other, body checking themselves out of the way. The act of forgetting is the machinery of remembering. Things move out of the way to carve an entrance for things to move in. We are just walking through space on something we think is the ground, trying to hold onto something we think is salvation and sinking slowly into the universe like ants in a juicy pile of bog-sand.

The only thing that mattered was seeing my mom, and forgiving her for not loving me. I was so ready to turn it around, to go back to school and "apply myself." To get a job. To let myself love people. To stop drinking once and for all. Finally I would map my life out and follow it, at least sort of.

I skidded back onto the road, marking my terror on the man-made ground. I wondered how mom could fit all the grief she had in her body. I selfishly wanted her to tell me it wasn't my fault, that my dad didn't die because of me. I needed some sort of reassurance. When my head got quiet, the real dread came in like nails on the chalk of my bones. I could feel my mother's absence ringing through me. So unimaginable were any words she could say to me. I tried to call out to her through the static in my car: "Mom, mom, mom, please don't cut off my blood supply. I know I'm going crazy now in the vat. I know that I'm losing all the things I need to be in touch with in order to make it through these week-long days. Tell me just once that it's not my fault." Unlike the melodic imagined conversations with Jordan, there was no response, I couldn't imagine her, and at the frequency I was losing myself it made me wonder if she existed at all.

When I got to her house I just stared at the long, paved driveway, the overgrown, dead lawn. My mom never liked people to know she was hurting or broken or even remotely human. I was sad to see the first evidence of some semblance of letting go, some lack of upkeep. I wondered what that must have meant for the inside of her head.

That wasn't the way mom liked to live. She had always had order. Her beige curtains in the windows, reflecting sunlight throughout the house, bright but not blinding. The blue door. With its brass handle. The flower beds in the front yard. Staring at the dark, worn-out house, the only thing that penetrated my senses then was the knowledge that my mom was in there alone with her grief, with her sadness, with nobody to talk to, nobody to ask her how she was. I knew how that loneliness felt and I hated that I left her with it for so long.

I never noticed before how sad, lonely and isolated our house was. It was just on the edge of the city. It didn't overlook anything beautiful, just a pile of pushed around dirt making room for the construction of more suburban bullshit. My mom loved it here because it was quiet. She needed the quiet because anything remotely chaotic cost her a lot more than anyone realised.

I sat nursing the lump in my throat. I couldn't remember the last time I'd eaten. or the last time I'd cared to. The preoccupation of my mind and gut was that I had to reach my mom now. I had to tell her that I knew what I knew and that we could talk about it. I could handle it. I had handled it my whole life, though poorly. After seeing Natalie I just wanted to hold my mom in my arms and tell her it was okay. That I wasn't just a man with an ulterior motive, that I was her flesh and blood and proud to be that.

I heard the soft pecking of fingernails on the window next to me and I looked at my mom for what felt like the first time on something like the eight thousandth day that I had known her. I looked at her face. Where my dad's laughter had lived in his, she had a regret that was inconsolable. Lines had been etched into her face by a grief that no one would ever know. Only those who had lost a lover would know this kind of grief. Would know the grief that sits in your bones. The grief that just sits there and gnaws at your enamel until one day you look in the mirror and you're translucent and all you are is this window for people to look in at sadness.

"Rory. What are you doing here?"

I rolled down the window, undid my seatbelt, slipping with the shaking of the hand that could move. I got out of the car and was greeted with no hug, no warmth.

"What happened to you?" She looked away from me, as always. I blamed my injured face this time.

"I don't want to talk about that. I have to tell you something."

Silence, and she wouldn't meet my eye.

"I'm sorry I didn't call you." I went on.

She looked at the ground and nodded, her eyes welling with tears. I sat there feeling guilty, met with none of the courage that I had premeditated. The time it had been since I last talked to her hit me all at once and I was suffocated by it. She didn't call me when my dad died. She didn't invite me to the funeral. I tried to stuff that all away so I could apologise to her for the way I existed, but some part of me felt resentful that I had to, or that I felt that way in the first place. She left me in the dark, encased in a loveless film far away from her and I was the one who had to apologise.

"I'm a coward and I'm not strong enough and I'm not as strong as you, and I'm sorry. Only now I think I understand what you've been through."

She looked straight at me, petrified behind her eyes. "Rory, please don't do this. I need you to leave."

"No, mom please. I get it, I know why you are the way you are with me, I don't blame you for it."

"Rory."

"It's alright, I was an impossible person, and the things you went through, God. I don't even know how you could bear it. You're stronger than I've ever given you credit for just for keeping me, for holding on so tight. For all the little ways you've made up for the things that happened to you. Mom I really need you, I need just five minutes to tell you how much."

"I need you to leave." She was backing away from me, looking at me with a horror in her face I never wanted to have actualised. "Get off of my property or I'll call the police."

"You're not serious." I stifled a laugh. My heart restarted in my chest, beating harder than it had been before. I wanted to look at her but my eyes pulsed in their frames when I tried. I didn't want her to see tears that she had caused, because damn her if she could look at me now and abandon me after all I had lost. She was my last hope for any kind of solace. My existence felt so bleak those days. I grasped at the sympathy I had for her as it frantically ran away from me. I knew I couldn't fight her on this. It felt like every time I got close to finally climbing over her wall, she added new bricks.

"Mom, I need you. I fucking need you now. I'm falling apart. Look at me. Please, look at me." I reached for her arm as she snapped it away.

"I can't do this with you, Rory." She turned away from me, heading back into her sad cave.

"You know what's fucked up, mom?" I yelled after her. "I came here to apologise to you. But for what? Really think about it. You didn't even call me when dad died. You didn't invite me to his funeral. Now I'm sitting here, half dead and you can't even look at me. What the fuck is your problem? I've spent my whole god damned life trying to earn your love. Why didn't you just fucking abort me then? Why do I even exist? Do you have any fucking idea what it feels like to be me? What you've done to me?" The tears were coming from my throat. This is not what I had meant to say.

She was standing with her hand on the doorknob waiting to escape me. She was crying hard and silently. "Please just go. You don't understand. I can't talk to you when you're like this."

"But I do understand, mom. I've known this whole time. You think you have this big fucking secret but you don't. I have seen some shit too. And I have spent my whole life loving and going without. "

"Rory *please*." She was hyperventilating. The words just kept coming from me before I could stop them.

"No, I won't stop. It's not fair. I understand what you went through. I understand it's hard to be without him. I understand that you're hurting, but do you have any idea what the fuck it has done to me? I'm a person, not a bad memory. A fucking person."

"Get off my property. Just get out of here. Please." She was impatiently wiping the tears from her face, her guard was up and I couldn't tell if she was seeing me or someone else when she looked at me.

"Please, mom." I was losing her ultimately.

"I don't want to see you, do you understand that? I don't want to see you. I can't handle seeing you right now. You have no idea what it feels like for me to look at you."

I walked back to my car, slammed the door and drove away, quickly and recklessly. I screamed over the muffled breaking sound of the radio, some happy-go-lucky CCR bullshit. I wasn't sure if I even liked music anymore, or anything for that matter.

I thought of Natalie. The memory of her came back into my ears with my raving screams of mercy. I couldn't save her, I couldn't talk to my mom. What the fuck was wrong with me? Why had I gone there and yelled at her like that? After everything she went through why did I do that to her too? I could feel Natalie choking in my own throat, could feel hands on her neck and on my own. I drove fast, pushing hard on the gas and enjoying the feeling of my skin breaking.

What use was I if I could never reconcile any of the hurt I'd caused? I just showed up on people's doorsteps to make them miserable. At least Natalie had opened up to me, proved that I wasn't such a termite. She trusted me, she helped me understand the things that no one ever explained to me. The way that humans can devour other humans. The crazy morbid way some behave. Why had I yelled at my mom like that? The one time I had her standing in front of me, I ruined it. I wanted to run back to her, beg her to give me some sign that I could make it up to her, beg her to give me just a drop of love, but instead I drove straight to my apartment dodging in and out of traffic, anxious to chase the lump in my throat with a quart of rye.

Chapter Eighteen

I'm running my nails over the spot on my neck where my throat would be, but I can't feel it. And I'm standing on the same street as always, the pavement cold on my exposed heel. I've worn my shoes down pacing this block. I know I won't be happy ever again now— I know that after seeing Natalie I can't run anymore. I cuss under my breath at all the people in the world who are able to turn their backs. All the people who are able to somehow morph someone's pain into something they can benefit from. I can't swallow anymore, and it hurts to think.

My mother hates me, my heart pounds in my chest trying to escape this pain. She despises and fears me. She loathes me at a frequency even I can't keep up with. And I can't stop seeing her face. My throat closes each time I swallow, punishing me for the tears I won't let out.

I needed to see Chuck. It was late. The bar might be busy and I can't stand a lot of people. Makes my skin crawl. All I see is little tornados waiting to fuck up my rhythm. I want to love them so bad, and in my mind, I chase people. Through my dreams too. I hold them there, special. Where they can't hurt me. I think of Ellie again. I think of her smile running away, screaming off her face when she saw that I haven't changed at all.

I think of how much I loved her, how it stayed trapped where everything else stayed trapped. I could only nod at her and hope she would find a way to unstick it from my dumb mouth. I wanted to tell her, howl after her: "Please don't go again, I would grow into my body a thousand times over just to hold you one more time. I'll find a way to shrink my skin to my bones and do it right. I'm sorry about who I am but you're the only person who's ever made me want to be better. And I love you. I love you so much it gathers all of me in my abdomen and sucks the blood from the rest of my body." But I never told her how I felt.

"Hard day?" Chuck, of course, was there, always reliable. "You look like someone put you through a meat grinder, kid."

"Fuck my body. Who cares about that damned thing?"

"So where you been?" He tapped his glass, asking for another.

Whisky placed in front of me, don't remember asking for it but probably did. I needed to get right to it. My nerve was running away, I tried to drink it down.

"I need to talk to you." My eyes were watering, whisky burning my throat-lump, sitting poorly in my mouth, could feel the nausea rising already.

"Alright. What is it?" He turned to me, concerned.

"My dad killed himself and it should have been me." My legs went numb. I didn't even have a chance to ripen those words on my breath, and I didn't remember thinking them. Another whisky down.

"Woah kid, you wanna get out of here and talk some?" Chuck.

"No. No. Sorry that's not– just forget that." Deep breath. "I just. I came here because–" Another whisky. Holding counter to catch breath. "What would you do if you saw someone, you know. Being hurt by someone?"

"You're gonna have to be more specific."

"Okay. I just. Alright. I met this girl, and to keep it short I saw her boyfriend beating the shit out of her and I don't know what to do now."

Chuck stared at me. "You don't know what to do now? Why didn't you do something then?"

"I already feel shitty about that, okay? I can't change it, so what do I do now?"

"There's not much you can do, is there?"

"That's fucking bullshit. I can't just know that's going on and then not do anything about it."

"Who is this girl? Why does she mean so much to you?"

"I don't know. She doesn't. She just. I feel responsible."

"Then do your fucking best. Find some part of you that hasn't been destroyed by your god damn nihilism and go do your best."

"Okay, but what does that mean?"

"That means that you can't save somebody that doesn't want to be saved. That means that she doesn't need you to save her but if you want to try, you'll get the fuck out of this bar and go try."

"I don't know how."

"Christ, kid. You can't just sit here and talk about shit, you have to actually do shit. Go fucking do something about it."

I left thinking of Natalie. I drove around thinking of Natalie and watched her building flit by in the corner of my eye five or ten times. I looked up and was parked in front of her house.

How could it be irrelevant that she's always on my mind? That she hollows me out more than I ever have been and that she reminds me of everything I've lost? But I've never seen someone so alive in all my life, maybe I could gain it all back. At first I think I'm in love with her but that fades and I want to save her. I want to save her so bad I start to feel like her name is my own. I start to feel like every echo in my spirit is a cry from her.

I sat there waiting for something to act for me. Smoking without remembering how many cigarettes I had lit off the butt-end of others. My throat was scratchy and dry. I could hear the air around my head buzzing, could hear my heart beating.

I got out of the car and walked up to the building. Realizing it wasn't even an apartment at all. It was a rugged old abandoned office building. Lacking the allure of a home, wind whistling through broken windows. I saw a man crouched behind one window with a needle in his hand, we made eye contact and I got back into my car. Too cowardly for this shit. Chuck said to try my best. What kind of feeble bullshit was that? Try my best? Empty pile of vowels and consonants. Waste of time. I drive away.

The last thing I said to Natalie was nothing. And why do I always express disgust or indifference to the people who need me most and love to the people who want no part of what I have to offer? I think of Jordan, how he'd know what to do about Natalie. Some people might say that he had a hero complex, I think he was just normal. Normal to want to protect the people who were in the most danger. He always did it for me. I acted like the only pain that existed in the whole world was my own. Like it was enough for me to just feel what had happened, and be sorry the rest of my life.

I threw myself on my bed, inhaling crumbs. Crusted pillow-drool rubbing against my face. I hear a door slam and someone yell: "Close your door you fucking idiot." The people in this building, they're so bored of their own shit they have to keep telling me how to clean mine.

I hadn't been sleeping at night and when I did, I dreamt of Natalie lucidly, so that it didn't feel like sleep at all but more like me running through a long old corridor trying to reach her before she concaved under a giant fist that flew from the ceiling like a big old bony spider. And would anyone even know? Where was her mom now, and her dad? He's really the one who did this to her. That fucking asshole, that selfish, selfish asshole. I hoped he was dead. I could see his fists and the shapes they made on her young body. I felt it happening to my own flesh. I was covered in goosebumps. I munched a stale bagel. I thought about showering, never actually did.

I had to find a way to break through my cowardice and confront her and her situation. Protect her. I had no plan, and I was too nervous of what I would find or not find. She could stay with me for a little while, sort things out. I could take care of her and maybe take care of me too. At least this way I spent less time drinking at the bar. And the monsters that sometimes chased me hadn't lately. Alcohol was becoming a quiet comfort for me again, predictable but hardly working. I made a bed up on the couch, laid out a towel on the table. It was sort of clean and sort of folded but mostly wrinkled and bunchy. I grabbed an extra toothbrush from the bathroom cabinet and put it on the counter, making ready for her. I had made my decision. I would go back for her if it killed me, I would not leave her behind.

When I was a little kid, my mom used to take me and Angela to the park. Sometimes I would hide under the disgusting snot-covered rocket ship and wait to see if she would come looking for me. She never really did. She would call my name maybe three times and then shout that they were going home. I tried not to cry every time, told myself that I was being an unreasonable little brat. I crawled out from under the rocket ship, felt the breeze of a soon to be rainy afternoon on my face, stinging my eyes. I couldn't tell if they were tears coming or a reaction to the crispness of the air. I watched my mom smile at Ange, hold her hand, run her fingers through her hair.

The tears came and I walked really slowly home behind them, waiting for her to look back and make sure I was tagging along. She never did.

I sit parked in front of Natalie's house, the cold air leaking in and freezing my limbs from bending. I think of calling Jordan. I imagine what he'd say: "Dude, let's go in there. I've fucking got this. Let's bust some nutters. But peacefully of course, all with love in the war." But that's a reality I'll never know because I am too embarrassed to call him and have been for the past four years. Is someone really your best friend if you leave them to go on some strung-out self-pity binge?

I stepped out of my car and got back in just as soon, realizing I wouldn't know what to say to her, wouldn't know how to take care of her. I'd never taken care of anything or anyone in my life and knowing who I am makes it feel like a bad idea.

I wondered about the state of her bones. I wondered if I was the morbid one for wondering so much about it. It's like if we can't see abuse we can pretend it's not happening. If we don't grow up with abuse in our own lives, then other people's abuses can just hide somewhere on the outskirts of us and we don't ever have to venture out to meet them. I was my own abuser though, and that brought me to her. Maybe saving her would teach me how to save myself.

Ever since I was ten years old I haven't believed that there's anything out there that can justify my existence. It only causes pain for everyone around me. It caused my dad pain and eventually was the thing that ultimately destroyed him, and it made my mom so unrecognisable, she couldn't even love me. She loved Angela plenty though. I knew it was just not for me, the love thing I mean. But I had some to give, some left over that mom wouldn't take.

Mother's Day was always a day of pressures. As children, we never had to worry about having creative intelligence because the little handmade gifts were picked out for us, and we had someone guiding us through the whole process. I fretted over mine so much that I started to sweat and shake. I cried every year trying to make my mom the perfect gift. One she would be happy to look at and be proud of me for making.

"Rory, it's okay. It's beautiful. Why don't you take a little bit of a break?" Grade one teachers have the softest voices.

"I can't take. A. Break." I glared up at her, eyes brimming, hands shaking. "I have to finish it."

She tried to take it from me, could see by the rate of my breathing that I was getting upset. "Sweetie, it's okay, there's going to be more time after recess to finish these. Take a break, do you want to read a book with me?"

I swatted at her hand and grabbed my work back. "No. Go away. I want to make my mom happy."

If Natalie came outside, I knew what I would do. I would offer her a place to stay, I would take her in. I knew that if she gave me a chance, I could really save her, really show her a different life. I didn't know what to do while I waited so I drank from my coffee mug, which incidentally was actually filled with coffee this time so I could stay alert and sober. That's when the tears started to come. Once they came they didn't stop. When my eyes dried up they started coming out my nose. I think with all the damage I'd been doing to myself my sinuses had compiled into one tube and all the grief and sorrow in me just drained out where it could find a hole.

If I couldn't gain the courage to go find Natalie myself how could I ever be brave enough to save her? The desperate tickle ran up and down my arm pathetically searching my limp body for some sign she was okay. I wished I could spread my care out in that moment and do something productive but all I could manage was to start honking my horn and as soon as the sound reverberated through my ears I sped away, afraid again of the consequences.

I knocked on mom's bedroom door. I'd had the nightmare again. Dad answered, I resented him for it as much as an eight-year-old could.

"Dad, I dreamt of the monster again."

Dad looked over his shoulder at my sleeping mother and closed the door behind him, crouching down to meet my face. "What monster?" he whispered.

"It's this guy." My voice was shaking. "He has claws for hands and black pits for eyes. Shark teeth. He chases me and says he'll get me. That he won't." Sob. "Give up."

Dad puts his arm around me. "It's okay Rory, it's just a dream, it's okay."

"Can I sleep with you guys tonight?"

Dad looks nervous. "How about if I come read to you until you fall back asleep again?"

I cry, hard. "Why can't I sleep with you and mom?"

Dad looks like he's going to cry too but doesn't give me an answer. He takes me by the hand into my room and tucks me in, reads to me until I pretend to fall asleep so he'll go away and I can stay up the rest of the night crying to the walls about my little misery.

I ran through the hallways of my apartment building, up the four flights to my floor screaming the lyrics to *Mr. Tambourine Man*, slamming my body against the walls and shouting back at the people who screamed at me to "shut my fucking mouth for god's sake." I yelled to slow the thoughts, blinked my eyes frantically to wash them off my brain. To block their entrance. I thought of my father, shouted at him through the roof of the stairwell. "You mother fucking asshole. What am I supposed to do now? What am I supposed to fucking do now? You left me with nothing. Fuck you. Fuck you."

My neighbor opened her door, "Shut the fuck up. What the hell is wrong with you?"

I yelled at her to fuck off. Slammed my door, threw up in the kitchen sink and looked for something to chase the taste away. I grasped mom, she flicked by. I grasped Natalie, she slipped away. I grasped dad, took a shot.

Chapter Nineteen

The dreariness of a child is typically non-existent. That is, small satisfactions linger enough to string together something like the only happiness we'll ever know. The melodic, slow beat of joy. Music filled my tiny body with ice, then warmed the nerves. A life alive in me like I had never known. I chased the sound, tripping over my tiny clumsy feet down to the basement. Fear had once lived in every corner brushed by darkness. Now all was alight, guided by my eardrums.

Dad loved playing guitar the way everyone ought to love something. He played with a fierceness that exists only in people who need an outlet most. Mom didn't like when he played because it meant that he wasn't readily available for her to bounce her never-ending list of worries off of. It meant that he was shut inside some capsule away from everyone else where nothing could touch him, and if he was unreachable then she didn't know how to hold on to anything at all.

Dad spent most of his days catering to everyone else. He held everything together, never stopping to rest or enjoy himself. That's why we made our secret pact. One Sunday of every month we would stay home from church, which took a lot of arguments from my mom no matter how many times we made our excuse not to come.

Half the fun was in making up the reason, the rest lay in the unknown pleasures we'd find waiting for us when the day came. Mom didn't like going places alone, she wasn't even all that religious, not at home. She would make it a point to go on Sundays and worship some invisible thing in her head. No one talked to her at church, or any of us for that matter. Angela and I would sit there uncomfortably. Mom would kneel on the pews and pray the whole time, sometimes crying, shaking a little, though no one knew who she was praying to.

I lived for those Sundays where the weird pressure and confusion was allowed to leave us. I loved those long talks with dad, where I felt like maybe I was human after all. He would teach me what he knew, which would end up being always my greatest lessons and my most painful memories. He would show me books that I wasn't able to read for years to come. He'd just sit them on the back shelves of my mind so that one day they'd nag me and I'd hardly know why. Stuff like Virginia Woolf,

Diane di Prima, Charlotte Perkins Gilman. He introduced me to poetry too, Allen Ginsberg, T.S. Eliot, Yeats. The stuff bounced off of me, but I just loved to hear him talk, and it happened to stay with me after all. Incidentally, dad loved talking to me as much as I loved being spoken to. It worked out quite well. We talked most about morality, and how it applied to almost everything. How our interactions with anything shaped the waves of our lives in some way, no matter how small the exchange. Especially when it applied to people. My dad tried to really get it into my head that any feeling, behaviour or silent non-verbal exchange with another human altered the course of their reality even if only by the tiniest fraction of a fraction. People respond to even slight connection, communication, even if only the slightest response that's hardly noticeable. The dramatics of everyday life were not the only things that shaped our realities, though they were the most apparent.

None of it made much sense to me when I was a kid, though of course he used analogies that might have made it easier, like slugs leaving trails on the earth, or the webbed, sticky fingers of frogs latching onto everything in their path. The interchangeable way that we all moved through life, half elegant, half unsure.

Every word my father spoke into my soul stayed somewhere tucked away, waiting for me to need it. When I needed to know something, the deepest inner voice of my spirit would speak up for me, and if it was quiet I would have to trust I wasn't ready for what it had to say to me. Most often there is no quiet in me, and when there is it usually means I'm shouting too loud in my head about things that aren't my business.

Things started to break apart in chunks that day, and in my recollection now it's the day that holds every fleeting good memory of my father. They all fly towards that moment to make a home in it. The way he held his guitar was unlike I'd ever seen anyone hold anyone or anything. We could exist just as we were, with time stopped for a moment. He was drawn to the response of the music the way ants crawl through holes in the ground to feed their young.

People understate and misunderstand music all too often. Music is the greatest alteration of time I have ever known.

When I finally reached my father, he looked up at me. "Rory, come sit with me a minute."

He patted a seat next to him, his right arm hung over the face of the guitar in its curved elegance.

"Any requests?" The glittering of his eyes was music enough, the way his wrinkles caught up with themselves in a way that only existed under the pressure of a smile. I felt myself begin to cry for a reason I can not express even now.

I didn't know the names of many songs, only the experience of them, the memory of a feeling they gave me that I didn't have a large enough vocabulary yet to name.

My dad started to play Mr. Tambourine Man. That was the first time I'd ever heard that song. He sang like there was no such thing as morning.

Ever since that day, Bob Dylan had a way of allowing me to be with my father again, even now that he was gone. He could stay there in that song, with me. That's the true magic of music, it stops time in both feeling and experience. It can transport you right back to a somatic, emotional moment with no noticeable shift in the state of your current reality. He played guitar less and less as time went on. These Sundays became fewer and further between.

I used to be afraid of growing up. When I was a kid watching my dad play guitar I wished that I could preserve those moments forever, and always felt sad when they ended because it meant that I was getting older again. Time wouldn't slow down for me and later in life I would learn to shove things down my throat to stop its forward motion but still, in the dead of dawn when everything was quiet and left over, I was getting older and my dad was getting further away from me.

Now I sit in my lonely adult life screeching my fingers along the neck of my father's greatest love. I try to feel his fingers, the sensations of loving him in my body, but he's gone. And it jumps around the room tormenting me with nothing to land on. I try to relearn some songs that I knew how to play in my youth. The sound comes out cracked, broken, no melody and too little pressure from my hands to strum the notes in a way that doesn't screech and burst the air. I breathe frustrated gasps, pushing and pulling on my longing to feel some reminder of a time when things hurt less. I feel embarrassed at the prospect that anyone might hear me. I feel startled at the suggestive agency music has over me. I feel afraid of it.

I sing the song anyway, in the broken melody it maybe was meant to be sung in all along. Mr. Tambourine Man. The instrument is not in tune, my voice is not in key, it's sad and far away. I can't feel the body that strums the chords, but I can feel the music. And I can feel my dad. When nothing else is enough, that is enough. That song is a time capsule. In it, we are forever locked in love.

Chapter Twenty

"I'm gonna call the fucking police if you don't get up." Some overbearing, preachy asshole was yelling at me. I sat up and stared him in the face. My eyes rolled over his lazily shaved jaw, his patchy eyebrows, his richman's toupee. He was shorter than I was, wearing a paisley bow tie and an ugly red tuxedo vest. I rolled over in the dirt and tried to go back to sleep.

My body started to tremble, I could smell the privilege leaking off his oily gross skin, could feel him leaning over me with the presence of one or two other people.

"What are you doing here? Get out." A woman's voice this time. I squinted up at her, the sun blotting out most of the features of her face. Under the crease of my arm, I was cradling my sweet amber baby. "Fuck yeah," I said as I took a long drink. I pulled myself off the sticky ground, sitting up, mud stuck to my sweaty face. Thirty seconds of confusion brought me the awareness that I was in a graveyard.

"You look like you need a drink." I said this to a woman whose hair was way too done up to match the fear in her eyes. The drama of these people, wiping the tears so delicately from their fake eyelashes, hoping to remove any trace that they were unwell, though a graveyard is an odd place to be concerned about such things.

I started laughing. Though I couldn't feel it leaving my throat, I knew it had to be mine. I looked down at the place I had been resting. "Ah, fuck." It read 'Robert Daley, 1945-2016.' "That's not my dad." I started laughing again. I felt a hand on my arm and my laughter stopped immediately. The toupee guy with the blotchy angry skin was glaring into my face.

"Hey, fuck off okay? I was just trying to visit my dad."

"I'm going to call the police." A woman shrieked. Another cried, "I just wanted to visit grandpa. Why do they let homeless people in here?"

I looked this one in the eye and said, "Who are you calling homeless? That's my dad. Well, it's supposed to be." I got off the ground. I felt someone's hands on me and started doing a waltz to get away. Chugging my whisky and calling them out as I saw them. "You guys have no idea what has happened to me, okay? I have had it fucked in my life. And you're all just dabbing your million-dollar faces visiting your grandpa who probably died very peacefully."

"How dare you?"

"And my dad? He didn't die peacefully, okay? He got fucked and then he fucked off. He just fucked off." I didn't want the tears to come. The woman in front of me with the pin curls was looking at me as though I were the nastiest thing she'd ever seen. "He is gone and he did not have time to prepare. And I did not have time to prepare. And now I'm here visiting your grandpa instead of him. So what kind of son does that make me? What kind? Fuck." I finished off the bottle and threw it at the walking trail next to us. It shattered and everyone screamed again. "You are all so melodramatic. Fuck off."

"Get out of here you dumb punk." Two guys grabbed me under each arm. "I strongly suggest you get some serious help."

"I can fucking walk, you know." I scoffed at them, pushing myself away from their grasp.

I dusted off my body and flipped them all off as I walked out of the cemetery. If you can call it walking. I hobbled. Slurring my steps. Those piss assholes. What kind of dicks yell at someone like that in a cemetery? They had no idea what I had lost. They had no idea how heavy my remorse weighed in the air of this graveyard. Who the fuck were they to act like the only people with a loved one under the earth? And they had time already to process it. A year had gone by. A year. And what had I had? A few months? Maybe. I couldn't keep track of the time anymore. The grains of sand in my shitty little hourglass were long since flipped over, losing him reset every day.

I bet they all had more time with their grandfather. I bet they all had a chance to wish him well. I had to believe that so I wouldn't feel bad. Though the hollowness in me wouldn't allow any more bad feelings. I was tapped out. I turned around once more to look at them. Now some of them were laughing, one was placing flowers down and a few of them were holding hands. How shitty and typical to be with your family in a graveyard. When my grandfather died my parents dropped me off at a babysitter's house. Angela went though. Mom said I would have caused a scene. And by this she meant certain people who knew enough about our family would whisper and make her feel self-conscious. Besides, my grandparents only ever met me once and I know they didn't like me.

Grandpa took one look at me and turned to my mom, with a disgusted expression concealing all the humanity I was told he had. I was nine years old. Old enough to understand that look meant he was expecting way more from me than I was able to give him. Mom barely spoke to her parents, even though she described them as close. Angela had a few vague memories of them, and I always wondered what caused the strain between everyone until the moment I met them. Mom probably told them how much I acted out. She used to call me a problem child. Dad would stick up for me but that would only cause them to fight. Mom was always crying but I heard stories through the blender of time that she hadn't always been like that.

Grandpa shook my hand briefly. The rest of the day we had spent sitting in the backyard, barbecuing food. Angela charming her way deeper into everyone's hearts and me tracing lines in an ant hill with my fingers, waiting to go home.

At least I can say my grandfather made an impression on me, mostly when he said, loud enough for me to hear, that my grandmother couldn't handle meeting me so she was out with friends. I wasn't glad when he died, but I wasn't sad either because for a few years I felt a keen resentment toward him. At least my mom tried to lie about how much she didn't love me. That man didn't hide it at all.

There were so many moments I lost without remembering where they went off to. I was tired of waking up places I didn't remember being, I was tired of snapping in and out of the past. I was so tired, but I'd be damned if I gave up now. All I really had space for was to go over the ideals in my mind. The ideal of my dad existing. If I spent time in the past then he was still there. Forever a part of me. If I focused hard enough I could still hear his voice, feel his tender touch on my shoulder. Imagine he was proud of me. Though I know he wouldn't be if he was alive now. He would never have shown it though, he would have believed I could make it out of this. Without him, there was no one to believe in me and I knew I would not make it out of this.

Walking down the road, I felt so infinitesimal, like it wouldn't matter to anyone else if I made it through so why should it matter to me? It didn't matter to me. The one thing I wanted to accomplish in going to school was completely wasted and the chance was past now. I just wanted to make my parents proud, but my mom would never look at me again and my dad was dead and I would forever be paying for someone else's crime.

Every time I closed my eyes I saw either my mother or Natalie. I saw their skin breaking. I saw them faltering there, under a tough facade. I saw myself walking out the door and betraying them. I wanted them to know that I hadn't given up. That I was still thinking of her and would be until I knew for sure that she was okay.

Natalie probably hated me for showing her a glimpse of salvation and then taking it away. I could have brought her out of that, I could have helped her and protected her, but I didn't. There was a frantic fear in my gut that told me I would never forgive myself for that. Knowing how much pain I caused just by being alive, how could I possibly think that I had justification to try to make my own life better? As though I deserved that. As though I deserve anything but to go back in time and abort myself.

I stopped at the gate. Couldn't feel my toes but not for a lack of warmth. I needed to see my father before I left. I couldn't be this close to him and just leave. I ran all over the cemetery, frantically looking for some mark that represented my father before I found a tiny little plastic peg sticking out of the ground with his name on it. And the realization of him being in the earth below me, away from this world was way too much. Way more than I thought it would be. I started to yell, and I threw myself on the ground and I begged him to talk to me:

"Come back, I know that death seems better. And I know that I am thinking about death wrong, but dad, I am dead too. I have died in my life and now my soul is a ghost and I don't know what to do but chase you and try to find you. The only time I hear myself laugh is when I can remember you so vividly my body can't help but make a noise." I groped the dirty ground, crying into the patchy grass, the freshly dug grave. "Dad, I wasn't even allowed to come to the funeral. How am I supposed to find you if I don't know where they put you? Where did they put you? Where are you? Where are you? Please just tell me you're proud of me.

Give me some sign you're proud of me, even when all I'm doing is laying in bed trying to be immortal as long as the day is long. But all of life is just one long day, and I know that you would understand that."

"Fuck dad, I miss you. I miss you so goddamn much and I hate you for leaving. And I know somehow you knew I'd feel this and you left anyways. Why the fuck did you do that?" My hands were shaking, on my knees in front of my father's grave. "You're not supposed to be here dad, you're not supposed to be here. You're supposed to be with me. What about me dad? I loved you so fucking much. The worst part is that I know why you did it. I've been hitting it hard in the soul too, it's not fucking easy out here is it? And what if I follow you under the earth now? Will you be mad at me? You were the only person in this fucked up unpleasant world who didn't make me feel like I had no place being here, like everywhere I went I was imposing and intruding. You were the only person who bothered to really talk to me. Other people, they maybe talk to "me" but you talked to me." I broke. My knees dug into the ground, my arm bleeding again from the pressure of my tense body. I felt a soft hand on my shoulder. The woman whose face was blotted out by the sun. She was sitting crouched next to me. We sat there silently crying. I wanted her to hold on forever.

Chapter Twenty-One

Accepted. Somehow, by some strange force, the admissions criteria didn't exceed what little I had accomplished up until that point. I had fooled the system somehow despite being thrown out of high school, despite having next to no credentials, despite being a drunk, sorry lunatic.

"Rory, that's fantastic." My dad said this to my mom instead of me, hoping that she would join in on the praise. She managed a smile before looking away at something else. "Isn't it great, Joyce? Our boy is going to university."

"Never thought I'd see the day." Angela rolled her eyes. I grinned at her, she winked.

"Well, yeah I decided I should probably make some use of myself, and I quit drinking too."

Mom got up, whacking her knee on the kitchen table, muttering under her breath while walking away from me. At any mention of my drinking, she left the room quickly. I thought she'd be happy I quit and was looking to turn my life around, but as usual, fighting for her approval was a painful and pointless task, like trying to preserve a decaying flower in a jar full of Draino.

I followed her into the living room. "Why can't you ever be happy for me, mom? Why does it always have to be some battle of wills with us?"

"I just can't keep up with your changing life decisions all the time."

"I'm twenty-three."

"I am fully aware of how old you are."

"Why can't I have this?"

"You can have this, just don't expect my support. Great for you, you decided to finally do something with yourself. Now let's see if you stick to it. I mean, come on Rory. You never follow through on anything you start. So don't blame me for not throwing a party."

My dad walked in the room, "Joyce, please. He's done a good thing."

The look she threw my dad summed up the whole conversation. It seemed to say: 'How dare you take his side? Have you seen him? He's pathetic.' She grabbed a bottle of wine from the table next to the china cabinet and stormed out of the room. My dad tried to pretend this was ordinary. "What are you going to major in?"

"I'm thinking philosophy." I appreciated the way he always tried to make space for me.

"Philosophy." His eyes lit up in a familiar way. I had always loved philosophy. In part thanks to Jordan.

My father played a much bigger part in my budding interest in philosophy. I'd never told him that, whether or not I understood it at the time. I tucked all the stories he told me in my youth away in a deep corner of my soul. They stirred sometimes when I knew there was something more.

How could I not want to know there was something more? To believe there was no purpose to existence would make mine too painful. If all it came down to was bodily pain (and that's all I represented to my mom), then I wouldn't want to go on. I did the equation in my head often. To believe I had come from some stormy nothingness would be a direct insult to the woman who gave me life, suggesting she had gone through it for nothing, that the universe was merely spitting on her humanity and dragging her around for fun.

Dad and I talked for an hour in the kitchen about great philosophers. I had never noticed how loud he laughed at my jokes. I felt good about myself. I could have stayed in that moment forever, but of course my mom had to come back downstairs, significantly more drunk than she had been when she left.

"Rory, I just have one question for you." She only stood so close to my face when she was on the edge. "What makes you think we'd be proud of you, after all that stuff you pulled? You completely robbed us blind emotionally."

"Joyce–"

"No, Patrick. It's my turn to talk. I want to know why this little shit thinks he can walk in here and tell me how to be a parent." "

"Joyce, please." Dad was standing between us now. "Don't do this. He doesn't deserve this."

"What about me? What do I deserve? I think I deserve more than a son who just causes me pain, a son who just walks in and out breaking shit and ruining my life and then expects me to be proud of him at the end of it all. Don't tell me how to feel, Patrick. Don't tell me how to talk to him. I can't believe he would think it's alright to come here expecting praise from me."

While she was talking, I watched a string of images play through my head: my own blood, the smell of a hospital, a tube in my throat pumping my stomach. Jordan picking me up, trying not to worry; Jordan getting angry at me for the first time ever. My self-righteousness, my self-loathing that burned everything I touched. The hospitality he gave me that I left behind. If I had abandoned anyone, it was him.

My dad started to say something to her, started to calm her down, hold her and console her, making my stomach flip over. I felt guilty for being angry at him for taking her side all the time. When mom was upset, no one else was even in the room.

The thing is, I hadn't fucked off on her to abandon her. I felt a sick sense of pleasure that she was so angry at me for leaving. Maybe if she felt abandoned by me that meant she must love me somehow in some way. Maybe I wasn't a complete waste after all. I felt insignificant in the room with her, but at least I knew now that she wasn't indifferent to me.

She would feel better once I proved to her that I was capable of changing my temperament. Once I finished school and made something of myself, I could finally prove I was worth her love.

She didn't know that I had tried to take my life, that I had been with Jordan and then without him and then off on my own, all by myself with my cigarettes and my self-pity. I removed myself from her life so that she could be happy. It made me sick to think that despite all my efforts, I wasn't the one who could make her happy.

I walked out of the room, where my absence wouldn't be noticed for hours. Angela looked up and tried to stop me but she knew the expression on my face. The sick dread in my navel pushed me forward, stopping for no one. If I couldn't do this shit right, if I failed, all my mother's pain would be for nothing.

Chapter Twenty-Two

"Excuse me young man, you can't just barge in here." The Dean of Students looked really uncomfortable, but what the hell. I had to do what I had to do before I lost the nerve. Words, translucent meandering floaters, missed by an abominable drunk, numerical as far as existence went, on cushioned leather-polished seats.

"Are you drunk?" He asked. I glanced down at myself, covered in dirt and blood, and imagined how obscene this must appear. The thought of how this must look to them gave me a sense of satisfaction. I didn't come here to scare anyone, but what else can you do when the answer is always a hesitant yes?

"I don't give a damn about any of this shit." This echoed unintentionally through the entire stuffy room. Honesty parachuted and fell to the floor, forgotten by greedy child-like ears who wanted only what they desired to hear and nothing less.

"I'm sorry, but who are you?" These suited fucks had no idea who I was. Why did I owe them an explanation? My body felt like a spoiled vessel dropping useless cargo on the doorsteps of all these people's stupid lives. What do you do with everything you're given when you don't want it?

The wisps of hair on my chin, patchy and thin just like my dad's. The only part of him that mirrored me. Those small fractions of self seemed to run mercilessly through my skeleton. Wandering with my brain in their hands to a place where I should have tried harder to be like him.

"I'm Rory Fucking Langford." I leaned over the Dean's desk and looked right in his face. "I'm sorry. I just can't bring myself to give a damn about this bullshit. So I am quitting school. Giving up. I'm out." I was tired of muttering under my breath, tired of wasting poignant moments on vials of vodka I'd pocketed from the liquor store. Little tiny baby bottles. Mindful helpings of poison to twist through my fingers and pour down my throat, nothing strong enough to keep the absinthe-like screams of expectation from my ears, but I tried. In due time, I knew the truth would have to pour from me that same place I had tried to swallow it.

"I'm sorry, are you a student here?" He looked nervous but held together by the hems of his suit coat. Thousands of dollars of self-control.

"Not anymore, good sir." I leaned in to shake his hand, he did not reciprocate.

"You know, you don't have to come in here to tell me this."

"Well I thought you might care about the people who pay your salary, silly me."

"Alright, then stop showing up. I think maybe this school is better off without you, in fact." He looked me once over, at my tattered clothes and dirty face. "You can get out of my office now before I call security. And don't worry about coming back here, because I'll make sure this decision of yours is final. Please leave. Now."

You can't deny yourself the simple pleasures of being who you are forever. Maybe for a little while, if you're lucky they'll catch you before you're muttering half-comprehensible regrets on your deathbed. Maybe to no one, maybe to the person who you've been cauterising your whole life. Who knows. I waited maybe three drunk seconds to respond to this.

"I just have one thing to say. I am fucking smarter than this shit." Fully aware of the way my temple throbbed as I hit myself in the head. I must have looked like a lunatic sitting there, swatting myself, trying to gain respect for who I really was. The reclamation of self can be a slow process, and what is it at the end of the day, if not the ultimate goal? Never having asked for this life, how can we be so eager to do what we're told? Are we sane enough to realise there might still be choice buried beneath these measly expectations?

"I'm fucking out of here."

"Okay." He seemed tired, looking down at his desk, picking up the sandwich he'd been eating when I interrupted.

I kicked a table as I stumbled out of the office, knocking a glass of water to the floor smashing at my feet. The Dean looked apathetic, as though this sort of thing happened every day.

My life tasted sour as my breath, on and off drunken binges. Forgetting to keep myself clean, having no reason to impress anyone or be impressed with myself, I wandered. Finding myself perhaps closer to who I really was after all was said and done.

There is no road map, so when I finally used my own free will to abandon the institution that housed me and babysat my ambitions, I did feel free. Before this decision, I tried against my will to succeed, called into office after office to negotiate my stability.

"You're going down a long dangerous path to nowhere." The school counsellor always spoke as though he was given some secret insight into how one should live their life.

"I have ideas." Trying to dredge up these ideas was always a daunting task. They never seemed to want to unstick themselves from my tongue. Maybe I only believed in them when we were alone together, maybe other people's opinions would put them in a light I couldn't bear to see them in.

"What kind of ideas?"

"About myself, maybe about the kind of person I might be."

"What kind of person is that?"

I glanced at his bookshelves: various surface-scratching psychology books and an outdated edition of the DSM.

"Maybe my idea is about finding out what that means."

A look of judgement.

"Okay. And how are you planning to figure this out?"

"Maybe I need to be somewhere I can think. I don't know if school was the right choice for me. There's too much space here for me to think myself into madness. I can't tell the difference between who I am and who I'm supposed to be, what I think and what I'm being told to think."

"Education is a very important thing. I wouldn't give it up so fast."

"Thank you for believing in me, but it's useless if I don't."

I would never be the perfect role model of a well-lived life. No struggle as long as you're contained in institutions that drive you to follow an unharmed path. A cozy nine to five. A family who loves you or at least can stand to be around you. A peaceful death with few regrets. No one knew what I was born from anyways, so what did their opinions matter?

And now I'm lying in the sobering grass, my tonsils vibrating, a two-six of whisky down the hole within the last twenty-four hours, and who was I now? And who was I then? And what did it matter? I was finally free.

Chapter Twenty-Three

I'm a useless piece of shit, Rory Fucking Langford and the pathetic brain dogs, shitting all over the roof of my mouth, calling it speech. I hate my dumb pandering mind.

Who signed off on the agreement to give me free will and a voice? Whose fucked up idea was it to allow me to think and feel shit? How could I not at least try to protect Natalie, offer her an out, show her that there was someone in the world who gave a damn about her beyond what they could gain from her? I felt so uncomfortable. She lived in a sort of thin substance in me, somewhere right at the base of my heart. I was full of her, the sensation in my chest, the sick butterflies, the twisted knots in my back.

I didn't sleep at night. I thought of my father

and then I thought of Natalie and then I avoided thinking of my mother. I had unwittingly started a drinking game with myself where every time I thought about my mom I would drink more and faster— to burn my throat, distract my senses, bring myself somewhere else. I wrote about Natalie and thought about Natalie incessantly. My need for her to be okay existed as a pressure in my own sternum for me to be okay.

The streets at night are beautiful, when everyone's quietly existing in their own misery or solace. Walking around, if you look up, you just feel so insignificant. You wonder how anyone can argue that they're special.

I walked all the way to Natalie's house. Somehow, despite my eyes wanting to look in two different directions, I made it there. By some grain of luck she was standing right outside, having a cigarette with a deeply mournful look on her face. I felt the air of the world suck into my body. I choked on it and stared at her for an uncomfortably long time.

"Natalie."

She came rushing over to me, her hair in mats, face sticky with old tears, voice raspy with desperation. She didn't say anything but her breathing was slow, her skin feverish and dry. I ran my fingers through her hair, we sifted through our realities to find a common ground. That shared loss that trickled from her to me and back again.

Her voice tethered down into a sweet and thick nothing. We walked through the night until the other side was morning. We knew then that our flesh could be soft and we could find a part of us on the dusty floors of our chests that would not hurt so much, the part that we hid away the night things started to go wrong. The part of us we whispered to that we'd be back for. There would be a ticking of time, wrapping around it in waves and vibrations and then in some semblance of sound and cosmic revelation we could awaken the part of us who survived by sleeping. We got in my car and raced away from everything we had known.

When I was a child, I used to walk back and forth down the street in front of my house with my mother's fingers wrapped around my tiny hands. I fell in love with the way they cooled the spaces between my fingers. The soft way they would let me know that I was okay. She wouldn't say a word, yet I'd strain to hear a sound. I returned home only when holding the wind in my tiny fist froze my hands and walking into the house would finally bring me a feeling of simulated warmth.

There was something so tragic and lonesome about the way Natalie moved through the world. It reminded me of watching myself walk down a dusty street alone.

She moved up to my face, the fleeting pictures of valleys and prairies, the cinema reel of escape ripped from my eyes as she asked me what I was doing. I blinked, quickly trying to reset my field of vision. Natalie was standing in front of me, a strange look painted across the face that had just been laughing next to me.

"Do I know you?" She tried to look at me but her eyes bounced away from my face every attempt.

"Sorry." I walked away from her, shaking from my asshole to my fingertips. What the fuck was I doing there? The space between fantasy and reality was shocked into a strange plateau too soon for me to formulate which was which, where I was. Whose hands were reaching in my pocket for my keys, why the hell had I decided to walk here?

I breathed through the apprehension and turned back to her. "Do you need a place to stay?"

"Um. No?" She looked uncomfortable, trying to finish her cigarette quickly so she could head back inside."

"I want to help you."

Now she looked scared. "Who the hell are you?"

I was starting to get frustrated that I had to explain myself, that she didn't just automatically get it. "I was there, the other night. I saw what he did to you."

She took a step toward me, her expression turned to anger. "Get the fuck out of here. I don't want your help, do you understand? I don't give a flying fuck about you. I don't want your fucking help. I better not ever see you here again, creep. Do you understand?"

I could feel the regret bloat in my legs as I drove away, but what else could I do? I couldn't make her accept my help. I couldn't make her see things the way that I did. I couldn't save her, so I was walking out on her again. I kicked myself for being a coward while my brain tried to argue with me: there was nothing I could have done.

I hit my head with my fist until I felt a distraction-headache strong enough to carry me home.

Chapter
Twenty-Four

That stupid asshole at the liquor store wouldn't sell me my booze cause I was short a dollar. A fucking dollar. These dumbass capitalist pigs think they can take every fucking penny to my name? No integrity at all. Don't they know I have a goddamn headache? I was pacing around the block. I couldn't act here, not at the store I just left from. It'd be too obvious. I went there all the time. So I headed to the next store down the street. Great thing about living near the party hub of the city is that there's a liquor store adjacent to every greasy donair shop. I wiped the sweat from my forehead, my heart beating in a strange way. The bell jingled, I avoided eye contact. I think the dude suspected something already. I didn't care, I needed the booze. If he was smart he wouldn't stop me, because I'd have done anything to make the shaking stop.

My head had a pulse on every square inch of scalp. My fingers wouldn't bend and my legs could hardly carry me through the aisles, everything blurred together. I hadn't had a drink in a day and a half. My heart would beat hard and then stop, hard and then stop. I felt like I was chasing myself through a long narrow tunnel, my body is moving a pace behind. The world kept stuttering. I grabbed the bottle, cradled her under my coat. The guy at the counter was texting. I watched him to see if he was watching me, my throat was closing. The sweat under my arm made the label stick to my skin. I walked as fast as I could out of the store. I don't know if that moron suspected anything.

There were cops down the street. I walked around the block, ducking behind buildings. I knew they were following me. That they could smell me from their cars, my stench stuck to their uniforms. They had a nose for people like me, trained to seek out the disorderly and put them behind their caged window, to mock and demonise. I wouldn't be exploited by them, though. I had ideas about escape that they'd never even heard of. I heard a crunch of feet on the gravel behind me. My fist clenched and I almost dropped my life, catching her before she shattered on the ground below me.

I was irritable at the man walking his dog. He looked at me, I suspect he might've been asked to look at me. Asked to follow me. Maybe I've done worse things that I don't remember. Maybe each path I tread outside of my house is bringing me closer and closer to the dizziness of incarceration. I peeked around corners, a car was coming and my eyes were still blurring, I could hardly hold onto the bottle, my hands were so wet and clammy. I couldn't trust that it wasn't the cops, or another man sent to follow me. I wasn't ready to put down my surrender. I chased myself through another alleyway, found my way home in a zig zag, confused route. I threw the booze into my throat and I'm home before I arrived at my apartment, my mom standing outside staring at her shoes.

"Mom. What are you doing here?" I tucked the bottle back under my coat, dropped the lid, sloshing whisky all over my side, pretending not to notice. I'm shaking now and she's looking at me like she could take my life from me. "Who told you to come here? Why are you here?" I felt my eyes start leaking. I need her gone, out, away from me.

"I just wanted to talk to you." She stepped away from me, another two feet to the ten she was already keeping between us. "I can go if it's a bad time."

"They're going to see us out here, just come inside."

"Who's going to see us?" Mom's worried, I could tell by the pitch of her voice.

"Come inside, for fuck's sake." I held the door open, my breath came out shallow and hard, it stuck to my throat, my body was soaked with sweat. "Come on!" I shouted at her but she's still standing back, deciding whether to follow me or run away. She took the plunge.

I put my arm around her and took her up the stairs, looking back to make sure no one was behind us. She moved away from me. I took a long drink, losing my balance, grabbing the railing to steady myself, forgetting I couldn't breathe and drink at the same time. The three flights of stairs felt twenty times its height. I didn't want to look at my mother. I didn't know if it was safe for her to go back outside, I didn't know if I was safe inside with her.

I fumbled with my key, put the bottle down to rest, dumped a bit on the ground, picked it up and kissed its open throat to apologise. Mom was staring at me— I could feel her heart beating across the floor and I knew she was afraid of me. "Mom, it's okay." I tried to reach out and touch her but she flinched. "I'm alright, sorry. It's been a bit of a weird day." Smiling felt unnatural, I could feel my face contorting and my eyes failing to follow along with the direction of my mouth. She didn't say anything. "I'm sorry mom, I'm a little sick today. I don't know, you know how it is right?" I don't know why I chose to laugh at that moment. I went back to the door, got the key in the lock and held it open for her to walk through. She was shaking. Her steps slow and nervous.

She sat slow on the couch, bending her knees carefully as though she was afraid she'd never be able to get up again. I watched her, taking in her features. Was there some universal, cosmic guidance in my life after all? And had it brought me my mother? She looked at her hands in her lap, small and delicate, wrinkled at the knuckles. Her eyes were big and sad like you'd expect. She reminded me of a child. I wanted to wrap her up and carry her somewhere safe. But I was afraid. She had more power to hurt me than anyone.

"You hungry? You want a drink?" I asked her, I took another shot. I was starting to feel more steady, more sane, and then confused. "Wait, why are you here again?"

She cleared her throat, her voice raspy and nervous. She stuttered. "I just wanted to know, I just wanted to tell you. That I was sorry. So I'm sorry." She started to get up.

"Wait, wait, wait." I ran over to her and jumped on the couch, sitting next to her. "It's okay, please stay. I can make you some food. Do you want something to eat? Maybe some pasta? I could make a salad. No, wait. I think the lettuce has gone bad. I don't know what I have. I could look for something-"

"Rory, I think I-"

"Oh, there's a grocery store not too far away, I could go there. Get what you want. I could make that pasta dish you like so much. I think I have some cheese in the fridge too. Whatever, I can buy that too. You wanna come with me?" I stood up to find my keys, she put her hand on my arm, followed me to the door.

"Rory, what the hell is going on with you?"

"I'm good, I just wanna make you something to eat. "

She stared at me. "Can I take you to get some help, Rory?"

"Help? No. I've just not been getting much sleep. Makes me a little loopy. You know how it is."

"I don't think you're well."

"For christ's sake, I'm fucking fine. Will you just lay off me?" I was starting to get annoyed. My mother never came to see me and now that she was here, I just wanted to do something nice for her and she wouldn't let me.

"You are scaring me." This was the longest she had ever held eye contact with me.

I held my breath, not daring to make a sound that might pressure her out of saying whatever it was she had to say. Finally, she felt something for me.

"If I'm scaring you so much, you don't have to be here." Everything in me wanted her to stay. My mouth was bleeding, I was chewing my cheek, my heart beating in my throat, begging for booze. It took every last thing I had not to scream at her to stay and never leave, ever again. I needed to tell her how much I always loved her and how she could fix everything wrong about me if she just held me one time like she meant it.

"I was unfair to you the other day." Her speech startled me, I was so deep in fantasy of her staying that I forgot she was still there.

"It's okay, mom. I understand."

"No, it isn't okay. " She looked around my apartment, the sight of which made her start crying. "I know you're not doing well. I know I don't know how to be there for you, but you're sick, Rory. You need help."

I tried to argue. "I'm okay mom, I promise. I don't want to be another thing for you to worry about. Just come and sit down."

I prompted her to the sofa while I made her a cup of tea. I wanted to stay in the kitchen far away from the conversation I had fallen into. I didn't want to look at her grief right now. It tasted like poison and it clouded my eyes. I didn't want to forgive her in that moment for the ways she had hurt me. I wasn't ready. But I also wasn't ready to sit with the guilt I had building in my stomach for not forgiving her.

"It's just hard now with him gone. But I want to try. I need you to get help."

This felt like a cop out in a way, a cheap apology that fell off her tongue and made no sound for its lack of weight. I wanted to scream at her. I wanted to tell her: "You have no fucking idea what it feels like to be this alien. To be treated like some slimy thing that keeps showing up on your doorstep instead of a son. I think it would have been better if you had aborted me because the pain I live with now just for being alive is too much and I don't know what to do with it." But what came out of my mouth instead was: "It's okay mom, you don't need to worry about me."

I think sometimes that guilt may be heavier than anything else. It keeps us talking to each other. It brought my mom here to me. It keeps me searching for Natalie. When my mom talks to me I can only see Natalie now. I can only feel her fingertips wiping the sweat from my head, hoping I'm alive. I can only taste the booze and the sad renditions of tears that come with and before it. I can only feel the unconsciousness that I rest with every day.

I wanted to tell her to leave. I wanted to tell her that her apology is no good to me. That the words were light. But I didn't believe that myself, so how could I lie to her when she was being vulnerable for the first time since I had been born? I sat down next to her on the couch, putting her cup of tea in front of her on the coffee table.

"I just want you to know that regardless of what I'm going through, you're a good man." She couldn't meet my eye when she said this. "You are not the past. You get to design your life."

"Ah, the ol' cliche 'I don't know what to say' pep talk." I couldn't stop the words from coming out that time. I think I wanted to hurt her.

"Listen to me."

"I don't want to listen to you, mom." I was crying like a child. She made no move to comfort me. "I appreciate that you're trying, I really do. I really appreciate you coming here to tell me you're sorry. But if it's out of guilt or some sort of obligation, I want to tell you now that it's removed. You have no obligation to me. I can take care of myself."

"Angela told me that you've been drinking again. I didn't know it was this bad."

"Did she send you here?"

"No, I came here at my own volition. I need to make things right with you."

"And how do you suppose that's going to happen?"

"I got a therapist. For us."

Silence, and then, laughter. "For us? You want me to just jump in talking about this shit to a stranger when you and I have never talked about it one on one?"

"We're talking about it now."

"Don't you think it's going to take more than one conversation?"

"You're drunk. Maybe we should talk about this a different time."

"I'm not drunk, I'm angry. I'm angry that you think it's my job to fix this. Why don't you go to the therapist and then if it seems to be going well, then maybe I'll show up and shake the dude's hand. But right now, I have a system."

"A system?"

"Angela told you I'm drinking again."

She looked at the floor, "I shouldn't have come here."

"No, you shouldn't have. Not for this."

I started crying again and she put her hand on my knee, quickly pulling it away. "I really, really want to be your mom. I always have. I just haven't known how."

"It would be better if you just continued saying nothing at all. I was starting to get used to that. But instead you come here and try to give me hope. That fucks me up more than anything. Stop doing this to me."

"I'm not doing anything to you."

"You can't even see it. "

"Can't you see I'm really trying here?" Tears were leaking so quietly out of the corners of her eyes that they seemed rehearsed.

"No, actually I can't. Please go now. I have shit to do."

"What do you have to do that could be more important than this?"

"It's none of your business. You've made it very clear that I'm not your son."

"I want to know about your life."

"You do? You want to know how I drink myself to blackout every day? How I get in fights with security guards, police officers, professors, random people in the street? How the only friend I have right now is a drunk old whack job at the bar?"

"What about Jordan?" She was trying to make this natural.

"Oh yeah, Jordan. You mean the guy I abandoned after he saved me from trying to kill myself?"

"What are you talking about?"

"You don't want to know."

"Rory, why do you act like this?"

"Because you pushed me away. Because you fucked me up to this point. I don't know how else to act. I don't know how to be your perfect fucking son. Stop expecting something different every time you see me. You can't just say sorry and think the hurt is going to go away. Where the fuck have you been? Where were you when I really needed you? I don't need you anymore."

"I can't do this." She walked out, slammed the door, crying. As she left, all I could think about was that I hoped she would still want to try the next day.

Maybe she had her reasons to have a hard time loving me, but I didn't want her to start now when my whole life had been some sort of convoluted mess of pain and guilt. My heart clenched like a swollen fist in my chest against the weight of her leaving even though I was the one who had pushed her out the door.

Chapter
Twenty-Five

I hadn't really intended to speak to Blake ever again, but sometimes the loneliness really sucks the balls out of you and you end up texting someone that makes you sick in your guts. My drunken, compulsive alter-ego really fucks me over sometimes. His band had a stupid name, Suture the Wound or some shit like that. I imagined a bunch of post-pubescent boys who all looked like replicas of each other. As if I'd go see a bunch of losers like that.

On my way out to the show I filled my flask up and shoved it in the front of my pants. I couldn't afford to drink at a bar and I couldn't afford to go see these assholes without a drink. The walk seemed longer than usual, like my legs were dragging against the pavement, shaking although it wasn't cold. I guess I forgot to eat again. The stomach ache alerted me, bile rose into my throat, the tangy sour taste of negligence. I found a squished piece of gum in the pocket of my dirty jeans. The sugar on my tongue made me more nauseous so I spat it out and shot my flask between my lips instead.

When I arrived everything was alive. People were talking high, excited to see each other, excited to see anyone. I bummed a cigarette off someone, he tried to make conversation with me, I shut him out and walked around the corner. I was borderline sober. Almost too sober to handle the commotion of the evening. I swallowed some saving grace, lit the cigarette and jammed my headphones in my ears. Keeping the music low and peering around the corner once in a while to make sure my hiding spot was secure.

How do people socialise with such ease? Talking to the people I know best is hard enough as it is. I guess I could see the appeal insofar as talking to strangers is safer. They don't know your story, they don't know the dirt you've rolled through. They don't know how many times you've been at the bottom of the hill begging for your life. I feel like I wear all this on my sleeve, feel the way people look at me, as though my head may roll off my shoulders at any second. The rapid confusion at the way I carry myself, never able to get comfortable sitting still. I shift my eyes around a lot when I talk, too self-conscious to rest on another person's face for long. I don't want them to look at me.

I heard drums, soundcheck. People cheered obnoxiously for little reason. I took a drag from my cigarette that burned through a quarter of it in one go. I coughed and my senses all blurred together. I threw up on my shoes. Motherfucker.

"Hey dude. Someone told me some weird guy was hanging around, thought I'd check it out. Good to see you, glad you came out." Blake was interrupting my socialisation ritual.

"Mmm." I replied, hoping there was some way I could keep his eyes from travelling too low and seeing how badly I'd failed this early in the night.

"You alright, buddy?" He looked down at my shoes, and back up to the glazed pits in my head.

"Yeah, yeah. I think I'm just gonna go home. Didn't know you were playing here tonight."

"We literally just texted last night talking about this show."

"Oh, yeah. I forgot."

"It's all good dude. You're good. Just stick with me. We don't go on for an hour anyway. You wanna take a walk or something?"

"Okay."

We started to walk but my legs quickly betrayed me, begging me to stop moving. I could feel the inside of my body deteriorating. Everything looked too bright, even the darkness. I didn't want to drink in front of him, had to drink in front of him, didn't want to blow my cover. Had to act natural, act cool. I didn't even realise he had been talking to me.

"... so I get what it's like having anxiety."

"I don't have anxiety."

"Okay."

"Can we sit down?" I couldn't breathe. Every time I looked at the world around me the air got stuck somewhere just below my Adam's apple. We sat on a curb, had only made it about a block away from the bar. "I don't think I can do this."

"Do what?"

Fuck no, I was not going to break down to this guy, this dumb hardcore kid with the tattoos and the nose ring. "I can't be outside right now."

"You want me to take you home?"

"Why?"

"I know I don't know you, but you seem alright. I wouldn't mind helping if you need that. You don't look so good."

"Yeah, probably not." My breathing was coming out harsh and slow. I kept forgetting how to do it.

"Hey man, it's okay. "

"I'm good, I think I'm just getting sick or something. You ever feel like you're not in your body?"

"When I used to do drugs, yeah." He laughed.

"I don't do drugs. I don't think."

"You don't think?"

Now I was starting to worry that drugs had got into my body somehow. Maybe all the pieces of my life I kept losing were taken against my will. Someone had drugged me. "I think I'm on drugs right now." I said.

"What'd you take?"

"Nothing."

"Well then, how could you be on drugs?"

"I don't know."

"They don't just come out of thin air." He was making fun of me, I could feel it.

"Yeah, I know that."

"Dude, what the fuck's up with you? My friend said you were lurking around just staring off at people. You're making people uneasy. You all good?"

"Yeah, I'm fine I think I just got slipped some shit."

"You been drinking?"

"No." I lied.

"Then how could you be slipped some shit?"

"I don't know."

"Okay, whatever. I have to get back." All the compassion he tried to hold for me had vanished. He was looking at me the way everyone did when I was actually honest. Excuse me for trying to come up with a reason for the way I felt. You probably would too if you felt this fucking strange all the damn time.

I reached into the crotch of my pants and pulled out my flask. Blake looked at me with apprehension. He looked around, uncomfortable.

I started to suspect that he was setting me up for something. So I asked him what he wanted.

"You know what man, forget it. You've obviously got a lot going on. I should help the guys set up."

"I thought you didn't go on for an hour."

"That varies sometimes." He got up to walk away, I let him.

I stared out into the evening. People all around me were chasing each other in blurs. I couldn't tell if I was drunk or sober. I drank more because I didn't know what to do with my hands, the flask was almost empty, I must be drunk. People walked by me in a breeze of motion but I couldn't feel their presence any more than I could see the wind. Conversations were lost and I couldn't hardly remember where I was. I had to remind myself over and over again what my name was. If my body hadn't been so heavy on that curb I might have been afraid. Maybe I should go to Natalie, try and talk to her again. I had a vague feeling she would understand this weird lead feeling I had in my chest. She might know how to fix it, or cope with it, or numb it out. Nothing that usually worked was helping anymore. I had to go back home, get more booze. I had to get to Natalie. I couldn't go see her. I replayed our last conversation in my head. I couldn't remember what parts of it were real. Had she told me not to come back? Or had she collapsed in my arms? Which was real and which was fantasy? I searched my head until my temples were throbbing.

The back of my neck was colliding with the base of my skull, I couldn't hold the heavy thing up anymore, couldn't think about her anymore. I threw up again, it didn't want to let go of my tongue this time, just hung off my lips like a clingy child. Where could I go? I needed my sister. I needed to go somewhere quiet where I could hide my face and plug my ears and pretend I wasn't actively participating in this world.

I didn't even have a handle on how to talk to myself in my head. My thoughts were spinning, my mouth tasted like vomit, my flask was empty, I had nothing to wash myself down with. I couldn't sit with my pounding heart, my knees were pulsating, my body was shaking and dizzy all the way up my spine. I needed a drink. I needed a connection. I needed to pretend that I knew what I was doing.

I trudged up the block again, slowly. Holding the wall of a building, unable to differentiate between what was anxiety and what was intoxication and what was a result of being too goddamn sober. My body didn't feel like mine, it was a stranger to me. I tried to talk outloud to myself: "Rory, you're alright." My voice came out like someone else's, far off and unfamiliar. My hands looked like hands I had never seen before. I held them out in front of me. I didn't want these ghost hands to touch my body. I didn't want these limbs to be attached to me. I used the hands to hit myself in the leg, see if I had a response in my brain, some proof that this weird vehicle I was riding in was mine.

It occurred to me then that I couldn't just take my body off, put it down, get out of it. I could only trick myself into believing that I was escaping my body when, really, I was stuck in it. I felt claustrophobic, suffocated. I couldn't breathe, I couldn't see. Everything around me was moving with the beat of my heart. Buildings were inhaling and exhaling, the street was rippling like a concrete river. I needed to get to someone, at least be somewhere public where people could witness if I was shutting down and put a stop to it. Maybe this was all in my head, maybe this sense of insanity was a work of my imagination, or a dream. I walked into the bar, looked for Blake, spotted him talking to a girl with pink hair and a moth tattoo on her forearm and went to the bathroom to throw up again.

Nothing of substance came out this time, just a gross creamy yellow liquid followed by a series of dry heaves. My throat was burning so I stuck my head under the tap and swallowed as much cold water as I could keep down. I needed to get someone to buy me a drink.

Before leaving the bathroom, I looked in the mirror, it was cracked down the middle and lined with stickers and graffiti. The person looking back at me had aged since the last time I saw him. The lines in his face were sunken in, the shading overdone. Scraggly facial hair outlined the tired frown lines, the cold empty eyes. I blinked a few times, he blinked back. He looked dead, terrifying, disgusting, his hair sticking up in all different directions, his mouth cracked and bleeding. An old yellow bruise healing under his left eye. I bent my fingers and moved them up to touch his face. The hand was scarred with pink lines and old gashes. I had foggy memories of stitches, blood pooling in my wrist, shattering glass. I don't remember when I had taken the bandages off, it must have been recent because my skin looked pale and afraid of the light.

I left the bathroom so quickly I tripped over the frame and fell face first on the floor, my flask digging into my balls. The people who saw it happen laughed. I dug the flask out of my crotch and slid it across the floor, stupid wretched thing. There were a lot of people around me, enough people that I could slip through and be immersed in a completely different crowd that hadn't seen me fall.

The floor was vibrating and some parts of it felt soft and melted. The place smelled as sticky as it looked. I went over to the bar and ordered a whisky. Blake was sitting there and said the bartender could put it on his tab. "Glad you decided to come inside after all." I don't know why he said this. He hadn't seemed glad about my presence at all when we were outside.

"Thanks for the drink," I said after slamming it down. He made finger guns as he got up to meet his band on the dinky little stage in the corner. I ordered another drink, poured it in my mouth without touching it to my lips, satiated and safe at last.

I looked over when I heard Blake's voice coming through a crackly speaker. He introduced his band and they started to play. I have no idea how they sounded because all the blood in my body plugged my ears when I saw the drummer. He was a disgusting, beastly looking fucker with matted hair falling in his eyes, and a condescending, pretentious expression permanently glued to his entitled face: Natalie's boyfriend, Max.

Chapter Twenty-Six

There's a terrible smell coming from somewhere next to me and I wake up to see Angela putting a bowl of soup down on the table. I hate drinking my meals unless there's something in it for me.

"What the fuck are you doing here?"

"What are you talking about? This is my house."

"Oh." I looked around, embarrassed. "Where are the kids?" The house was quiet, could hear a low hum of a washing machine. The couch cushions I was laying on were sliding off, two more inches and I'd be knocked right into her disgusting soup, hopefully too unconscious to have to eat it.

"John took them out for the afternoon."

"To keep them away from me, I bet."

"No one said that."

"You didn't have to. When's the last time I saw your kids? You don't trust me around them."

"When's the last time you tried to see them?

And you know what, maybe I don't trust you around them. Do you really blame me?"

Angela's kids were perfect little versions of her and her husband. They were so irritatingly mild-mannered and well behaved. I couldn't relate to someone like that.

"Whatever. I gotta go." I sat up, moving slowly as the room shook in my eyes.

"You absolutely do not. You're going to tell me what the hell happened to you last night and why you turned up here all beat up and angry."

"What? I didn't."

"I've tolerated a lot from you but I'm not putting up with this anymore. I have kids. I have a family. I have a job."

"Okay, okay. Holy shit. I get it. I don't need the fucking master list of all the ways you're better than me."

"Not everything is about you. You're a disaster. You can't expect people to just be okay with that. It's intrusive on our lives."

"Whose fucking life is it intruding on? Fuck you, I'm out of here."

"No wait, wait, please no. I'm sorry." She put her hand on me to stop me from standing up.

I felt ashamed of myself for putting her through this again.

"You came here last night pleading for me to help you. Don't you remember?" She pointed at her door as I shook my head. "You were standing right at that door. You were covered in blood and snot and you were crying like a maniac about some girl. I don't know what's going on with you but if you're going to show up here like that you better tell me. Rory, people care about you. Let us in so we can help you."

"I don't remember." My face felt hot, tight, insides full of ice. What did I do to Natalie? Why do I always black out when I need my memory the most? "I have to go."

"You're not leaving. We're going to get you help. Like, today."

"No, you have shit to do, kids and all that, remember?" I grabbed my coat, dragged my dizzy half-limp body to the door.

"Don't be condescending right now. I'm worried about you." I turned to face her.

"Wait a second. You called mom."

"Yeah, I did."

"It's your fucking fault that she came to my house and trashed everything."

"Trashed?"

"She threw a fit."

"She said you threw a fit."

"Whatever. She came over to lay some guilt on me and then left."

"She's trying to help."

"I don't give a fuck what she's trying to do. What's your problem? Why would you call her? You know how it is with us." Maybe I was trying to start a fight with her so she would kick me out. I knew no matter how much I begged to leave, my sister would try to play the diplomat. I tried to focus on what Angela was saying but I couldn't let any sound linger in my head for long. I had to think, had to remember the night before. I remembered the bar, the disgusting hungover smell of the bar, Blake trying to get me to come inside, my shoes covered in puke. I looked down at my shirt, dried vomit. I looked at my hands, they were swollen again, like this nightmare wouldn't ever let up. I'd never get my body back, maybe. What the fuck did I do? Maybe I really should stop drinking. Maybe I really should take my sister's help. I couldn't afford to lose these chunks of my life when Natalie was at stake now. Max. Max had been there. That was the last piece I remembered.

"Are you even listening to me?"

"No. Ange, I really have to go and fix some shit."

"You can't just keep walking out on everyone like this. I'm not going to let you leave again." Her voice broke and she stopped talking. I think she was more scared of my deterioration than anything else in the world.

"I'm not dad, Angela."

"I can't lose you, I can't handle it."

"You have mom."

"Oh please. Don't give me that 'poor me, mom doesn't love me' crap."

"Forget it. I have to go."

Though I said this, I made no move to walk through the door. I wanted her to convince me not to, but she didn't. She just stared at me, angry and concerned, and waited for me to follow through. Her worry wasn't enough yet. It felt too obligatory to be believed. I couldn't waste any more time trying to manipulate people into loving me. I had to figure out what went wrong and try to piece my night back together.

"Rory, please don't go. Please, I need to know where you are. Don't go. You can stay here a while if you need to. You can drink in the house, just please don't leave."

"You can't help me. I want help, I do. I don't want to be like this anymore, but right now there are more important things going on that I need to worry about first." I stepped into my vomit shoes and tried to leave.

She blocked the door. "I'll come with you then. I'll help you fix it."

"No. I'll come back if that's what you really want but I have to go now." I was becoming panicked.

"You promise you'll come back?"

For the first time I looked my sister in the eyes and made her a promise I had every intention to keep. I did want to come back. I did want to clean up, especially when I looked around at her perfect cozy life. I wanted her to teach me how to have that. I wanted her to teach me how to be part of something. She moved from the door without looking at me. I could hear her sad gasps as I walked away from her. The thing in me that would have normally felt something about her sorrow was sleeping still, or maybe it was dead. The only thing I could think about was having a drink, was moving away. Was running until my swollen body shut down completely. Natalie could be dead by now with all the hours I had lost. Every part of my body that had once had a capacity to care about anything else was all caught up on her.

I didn't want to keep hearing people reason with me that my mom did love me, that I was just in a mood and couldn't see it. If this was love, I didn't want it. I know that it's possible for parents not to love their children, not the way they should anyways. We're human and we can only do so much.

I kicked myself for showing up at the doorstep of the one person who cared the most about me in the world. How was I supposed to hide these things from her if I kept doing that? What kind of a coward was I to seek salvation when I ought to have been giving it to someone else? And if Natalie was really hurt because of some stupid ass thing I did, I don't know how I could ever forgive myself.

I just wanted everyone to leave me alone so I could continue on my slow decline. I wished that when I got drunk I didn't meddle so much in my own life, that I didn't talk to other people or fuck with their lives or show up anywhere remotely civilised. I couldn't believe there was once a time when drinking had been fun.

Maybe I should stay sober for Natalie, so that if I do see her again, I can have a clear indication of what I should do. Even though she said she doesn't want my help I knew that she needed it, she needed someone to do something. People couldn't just stand back while her boyfriend beat her like that. When I closed my eyes I could see the blood leaking out of her nose, when things were silent and I was sober I could hear the crack of a fist against a face and I could only see my mom and me and the beating of my heart in an ultrasound machine. I hated myself for being a product of my own life. I wanted to run my fingers across Natalie's face and fix everywhere she'd been broken. I wanted to stop the tears from my own eyes from stinging my wounds. I was a scrapbook of my own shit. I couldn't hide from anyone if I wanted to.

I looked in the rear-view mirror at my face: swollen, cracked, bleeding, I could hardly remember the last time my face didn't look this way. Shocked that I had even made it here in one piece without crashing into something, killing myself or someone else, or being pulled over. I laughed at my immaculate park job, wondered who my drunken self was and what he did when I wasn't around. I thought of what Jordan had said, about alcohol making it impossible to know yourself. I yearned for him, for his insights, to have it all back again. The times when there was a person I wasn't embarrassed to exist in front of. All I knew was that I had to make sure Natalie was okay.

Chapter Twenty-Seven

Blake's house was suspiciously nice. Maybe the little shit still lived with his rich parents. I had to believe he wasn't a freeloading douchebag, that he wasn't like Max, otherwise I wouldn't be able to keep my temper down long enough to face him with the facts that I needed him to know. He hadn't said much when I reached out to him and said I needed to talk. He invited me to his house, or whoever's house this was. I was sick to death thinking about what details from that night he might subject me to that my stupid drunk brain was trying to protect me from.

I kept sober that day because I didn't want to lose anyone's trust before I got a chance to earn it back. I wore my dad's suit coat because on a day like this I needed him to help me figure out what the fuck to do.

Little things were starting to come back to me, but they all felt unreal. I remembered being on stage for some reason or other. And I remembered Max hiding his face like a coward. I remembered being thrown from the bar. I could only write the missing details in my head, there was no way to know for sure.

Blake came outside and invited me to sit on the step with him. He was almost as bloodied up as I was. My heart sank so low I felt it poke the rim of my ass. Sober confrontation always made me feel like I was going to shit my pants. We sat in stone cold silence for a few minutes, both of us gathering whatever courage we needed.

"What the fuck is your problem man? Why did you have to do that?" My heart stuttered when he spoke. The hangover of sobriety was starting to leak into my bones.

"I'm really sorry." I was trying to keep my breathing steady, I played with the threads on my ripped jeans. I didn't want to admit to him that I didn't remember anything from the night. In admitting that, I would have to risk sounding like I couldn't take any accountability for whatever I did. It's hard to take the blame for something that someone else did with your body. When I got drunk I became a different person, embodied completely by all the anger and betrayal I had ever felt. That was me, in the deepest sense. I wasn't ready to admit that I had anything to do with that guy.

Blake laughed and looked away, and I could tell he was trying to suck back some rage so we could have a level-headed conversation. I decided to go with the facts that I did know for sure.

"Look, it's just that Max guy. I just can't stand that fucking guy."

"Yeah, you don't say."

"He's an abusive dickbag."

"If you're talking about Natalie, you have no idea what you're talking about." He moved to look me in the eye. "Max is a good fucking guy."

"No, he isn't. I know you probably have some stupid bro code where you defend each other so your shitty band doesn't break up, but you can't really stand by and defend your friends when they do shit like that."

"Natalie exaggerates. She probably told you some bullshit story to manipulate you. That's what she fucking does. She makes shit up."

"She didn't tell me anything. I fucking saw it."

Blake stood up. "You didn't see shit. You attacked Max in the middle of our set. And you really think people are going to believe that there was a reason for that? You're a rowdy drunk. That's the bottom line."

I stood up to face him. "Fuck you, man. You're

really gonna stand by while your friend abuses his girlfriend? Is that the kind of man you want to be?"

"Why does it matter to you so much?"

What a stupid fucking question. That should be obvious. Maybe I wasn't a fan of my own reality but when someone else was getting hurt I couldn't stand by and ignore that. I thought of my mom and my entire body weighted down into the earth. I didn't want to cry in front of this insensitive prick but the tears were rising in my throat. I tried to swallow them down and I heard them crackle beneath my neck.

"If you wanna fuck Natalie you can just ask, you know." He was trying to provoke me.

"So now you're not playing the nice guy because there's no one around to applaud you?" We were standing inches away from each other's faces.

"You're fucking crazy dude. You need some serious help."

"You're not the first person to say that to me."

"Is that supposed to be your way of defending yourself?"

"No, it's me standing here today telling you I'm not fucking afraid of what I am. I'm not afraid to stand up to nutsacks like you. I'm not afraid of admitting that I might be a bit insane. You should be afraid of how deeply you avoid what's right in front of you."

"Natalie's a fucking bitch. If anyone's abusive,

it's her. She leeches off him and cries to him about everything."

"He beats the shit out of her."

"Why would I believe that? I've known Max my whole life. I've met you twice and both times you were completely fucked and acting like a freak."

I spat in his face and walked away from him. He yelled after me: "Stay the fuck away from me and my friends."

I had to get home. I just fucked up so bad with Natalie. I just fucked up so bad. Maybe I really did imagine it all. I tried to remember what she looked like, someone honked as I swerved away from their car, remembering I couldn't drive with my eyes closed. I needed a drink. Needed money. Maybe Angela would give me some money. I couldn't function sober, and she wanted me to function. She wanted me to be well but I wasn't well like this. I don't know why people asked me to stop drinking, did they have any clue how fucked it was when I tried to do that?

I drove to Angela's house in a complete panic. Road was blurring, hardly remembered to stop at red lights. The radio was on high but I couldn't hear it. I could only hear an incessant buzzing in my ears that sounded like hell. I felt cold. I looked down at my knuckles. They were swollen, crusty and infected. But I hadn't attacked Max. Blake was a lying son of a bitch. I tried to focus on my body, to figure out which parts of me might remember what happened.

I had attacked Max. I saw him and I threw my glass to the floor. I lunged onto the stage, I jumped on his drums and tried to strangle him. I could feel my fingers on his fat little neck. I could see his eyes in their shocked disbelief. He didn't remember who I was. I had just a blind impulse and a thirst for revenge. I wonder if Natalie was there, if she saw what I did. I wonder what she was facing now because of what I'd done. The best I could hope for was that he was afraid now of retribution. People like that, they find any excuse to keep being a piece of shit.

Blake had tried to intervene. I was frozen in time, threw a cymbal at his face that sliced his cheek open. Bouncers were on us before anything could escalate further. I didn't get a single punch in. Those fucking assholes won.

I pounded on Angela's door frantically and she opened it looking startled. "What the hell, Rory?"

"I need some money," I panted, couldn't catch my breath. I couldn't feel my body, my heart was beating too hard. "I need some fucking money now, Angela. I'm dying. I need money. Please give me some money. Just like twenty bucks."

"No."

"What do you mean, no? I'll pay you back. Come on, I fucking need it, Angela. Don't you give a damn about me? Give me some fucking money I swear I'll pay you back. I swear to you I'll pay you back."

She walked into the house and brought out a five dollar bill. "This is all I'm giving you. Don't ever come here asking me for money ever again."

"Thank you, thank you, thank you." Enough for a beer. That would tide me over until I found another solution. I ran down her front steps.

"Wait Rory, where are you going?"

"I gotta go, I'll be back."

She slammed her door without saying anything. I wanted to care that she was fed up with me but I was too happy, could already taste the beer. Needed to get there as soon as possible. My body was contorted inside, I needed to even myself out. "I got you," I said to myself. "I'll take care of you now." I imagined Chuck laughing. The traffic lights blurred by like time was moving in fast forward. I tried to keep up with my surroundings, but I couldn't tell if I was moving forward, backward or crying too hard to know what was going on around me. Everything was a mess; the world was dumped out all over and the pieces flitted by like a montage of all the tragic endings of sad movies. I saw ghosts in the rearview mirror, headlights blinding me, I didn't know what time of day it was.

What would Jordan say, what would Chuck say? I couldn't hear anyone in my head. The pounding was ceasing, I was finally finding peace. I was dying. There were horns blaring in my ears. I opened my eyes. I was parked at a red light. Had to make this stop. Didn't know where I was. Turned into the adjacent parking lot. The holy church of booze bottles was right there. God brought me to my revival. I could make it through.

I shook while I walked, sweat pooling in the backs of my knees. I wiped droplets of salty desperation out of my eye lashes and looked for something I could buy with five dollars. Single beer. Pilsner. Fucking disgusting. How could I care? There were sober people out there and I was one of them now and I couldn't afford to be picky, didn't want to be one of them. I couldn't hear the cashier speak. I threw him the money. Told him to keep the change. He said I was short ten cents but I walked out. Saw Natalie walking toward the store. It's strange, the synchronicities life brings you when everything is fucked. The world came back into focus. I tucked the beer into the pocket of my dad's suit coat and walked up to her.

She stopped me from speaking before I could even think of what to say. "Stay the fuck away from me. Don't even think about coming near me." She reached her hand into her pocket, probably to pull out the infamous knife.

"No, it's okay. I just want to make sure you're okay."

"Why do you turn up everywhere? Why can't you just leave me alone?" She was crying. I tried to move to comfort her, she stepped away from me. A stand-off in the parking lot.

"I'm sorry I just want to make sure–"

"Yeah, that I'm okay. Fuck you, you stupid piece of shit. I'm leaving Max, okay? So leave me the hell alone. It's done, over. I'm staying with a friend. So stay the fuck away from me, because you're no better than he is."

I stopped trying to approach her. I stopped everything. She walked past me, confirming all my worst fears with the look of animosity in her eyes. She walked into the store and I stood there until someone honked at me to get out of the middle of the parking lot. Leaned over to dry heave, cracked the beer, tossed it down and was on my way.

I'm no better than Max. I'm no better than my dad. I'm no better than the vomit on my shoes. Piece of shit, Rory, you're a fucking piece of shit. I couldn't help weeping out loud like a scared child, screaming to the foggy windows of my car about my relentless self-loathing.

I needed whisky, I needed whisky fast. I couldn't stay in this body without it. I couldn't survive this anymore, it was too much. I had no money, no one to ask for money. I had to sell something. I didn't own anything. I parked in front of my apartment building, crying into my hands, snotting all over the steering wheel. The only thing I could think to sell was my father's guitar. It was the only thing I owned in the world, the only thing I had left of him. It didn't matter anymore, nothing mattered anymore because everything I ever fought for turned out to be a failure. "I'm so sorry, dad. I'm so fucking sorry. Please forgive me. I'm so sorry." Tears leaked all over his coat, echoing his departure in the shapes they made.

Chapter Twenty-Eight

"I mean it dude, my mom doesn't love me."

"How could you even say that, of course she does." Even Jordan couldn't look me in the eye when he said this. Everyone could see it, but none of them wanted to make it known how obvious it was, how painfully obvious it was that my mom didn't treat me the way a mother should.

"There's something you don't know."

The weight of my entire existence was a throbbing anchor in my gut, it held me down and battered me daily and I couldn't see through the other side anymore. I needed someone to help me carve some sort of entrance or exit out of it. I needed someone to carry the weight with me, but no one ever held my trust so clearly in their hands.

No one but Jordan, who had known me so well for so long, who had been put through the shit too.

He looked at me attentively, no resonance of a joke dancing on his face. He knew this was serious.

"My dad isn't my biological father."

The room shrunk when I said it out loud. I felt isolated in what remaining air there was around my head, but couldn't seem to breathe any of it in. Jordan didn't speak to tell me to go on, I could tell he didn't know whether he really wanted to hear this or not.

"Joyce, I know it's hard, but we can see this as some sort of redemption."

"I can't do it Patrick, I can't have this child. I can't be reminded every day of the fucking thing that happened to me. What if he looks like him?"

"You don't have to have the baby. We can go to the clinic if that's what you want. If you want to keep him, we can keep him. Everything is your call."

"Rory–"

"No, just let me say this," I said, and then continued. "My mom and dad, they thought a lot about whether or not they wanted to keep me. I personally think they made the wrong decision."

"Dude seriously, I know that shit is fucked but you can't carry it, it'll fucking kill you to carry the weight of that."

"You think I don't know that? How can I help it though? I do carry it." Jordan wasn't getting it. I knew he didn't want to. That the horror that brought me into this world was too much to bear, even for someone who didn't have to bear it.

"Joyce Langford?"

She walked into a small room, sat down and felt her heart beating in all the parts of her body she wished were numb. The nurse would have to examine her. She was given a pamphlet, what to expect after the procedure, the days of hell she might have to endure. She didn't want to feel her body, didn't want to endure any more. The fee was so high, too. Could she justify this procedure? Her mother had always told her everything happens for a reason. She always thought that was bullshit. But if she let it be true for now, maybe she could deal with all of this later. But she couldn't do that. She needed this gone, this thing in her. She didn't want any attention drawn to her body. She didn't want to feel it swell. But then she'd be alone with the memory, that dark night would never leave her.

She wanted to kill every part of it, including the tiny parasite. "I'm just going to examine your cervix, can you lay back for me?" The nurse tried to sound gentle, but the room was cold, and she couldn't make her body do what she wanted. Just as soon she was being asked by my dad, "Everything okay? That was quick."

She moved to sit next to him, couldn't look him in the eye. "I couldn't do it Patrick. I just couldn't do it. I'm so sorry. I know you don't want to keep him. But I just couldn't do it. I just couldn't." She broke in dad's arms, he held her as her legs gave out and stroked his own tears through her hair. "It's okay, love, it's okay. I want whatever you want. Whatever you need to heal."

"I don't know what I need. Just take me home."

Jordan watched me carefully, afraid I would explode into a million pieces and disappear, and if I had it my way that's how it would have played out.

"I don't think she was prepared for me to actually be a human breathing thing."

I sat there with my mom's truth on my tongue, glowing white hot. I felt embarrassed that I had come out of what happened to her. I felt absolute disgust at myself for taking up space anywhere I went. I was the object of complete and absolute terror. I was the human reminder of the evil that men do. Sometimes I touched my own skin and I could feel what he did to her in my body, the images played in my face. I dreamt at night that it was me attacking my mom and I woke up with puke on the sheets next to me, cursing my body for laying on its side, wishing I could choke on my own bile and not wake up. All the same, waking up from the dreams was the only salvation I ever got from the pain of existing. Some nights I was too afraid to sleep. I dreamt that there was a man out there with my face, attacking women. I thought about it too hard when I was awake, and I was that man. I was a part of him, I carried it in my blood and I wanted to kill it.

"Patrick it hurts. I'm afraid to look at my belly. I'm afraid to touch it."

"You can change your mind anytime, you don't have to go through with this."

"I can't. It's too late."

"We can get through this, we can get through anything." Dad knew this was a platitude, he hugged her, feeling ashamed. He blamed himself for working late the night it happened.

Jordan tried to remind me that the man who

raised me was still my father, but I couldn't hear it. DNA would say that I'm half of a monster. The ghost of one. A replica. Every time my mother looked at me I could feel what happened to her. She didn't love me so, I couldn't either.

"Man, let's just watch a movie or something. I don't want to talk about this depressing shit."

"Rory, listen. I usually don't want to shove advice on you but I really think you should talk to your parents about this, maybe go home and have a conversation about it."

"I can't. I have caused them too much pain already. I can't put her through that anymore."

"This is a lot to live with, you can't just carry it by yourself expecting it to go away. It's not going to. You have to deal with it. You have to process it or it will process you."

I didn't want to feel like a raw open wound, like a disease that my mom had contracted that, once extracted from her, developed into a human being that did nothing but remind her of her pain. I didn't want her to know that I knew. I was more afraid of her being hurt than I was of anything in the world. There were moments when I thought things might turn around, when she laughed at something I'd say, but then it was as though she had a snap realization and instantly stopped, distracted herself, went away from me. We could only co-exist in those moments when it was forgotten who I was and where I came from.

Jordan gave me a pep talk I could only half hold onto. We got into his car and drove for hours as the light of day faded away from us. I felt like he wasn't hearing me. I didn't want him to make it better, I didn't want him to feed me some positive shit that would undo all the pain I felt. I just wanted him to look at me and say that what I felt was justified and that he understood. I wanted to be my own person but I shared physical parts of him and that disgusted me. And until she could look at me with love, I couldn't look at me at all.

I wanted to go back and erase it all, make it different for her. Tell her to take a different way home, tell her to never leave the house, tell her to hide away and make me not exist.

We try to redeem in ourselves the things that were done to us, but it's not our job. It was never my mom's job to carry the shame that I brought into the world. I wanted to kill the man who did this. I wanted to kill the parts of me that resembled him. I stared out the window of Jordan's car, watching other people's lives flicker by. I tried to root myself to this moment with Jordan, where someone accepted this morbid detail about me, but I couldn't just tuck it away into the night. I couldn't sit right until the thing in me was dead.

Chapter Twenty-Nine

I knew it was wrong. To rob my father's soul for the purpose of my own gratification. I needed it to stop. I needed to beat myself to death with it. That beer hadn't done it for me, I needed something stronger. Something that would burn me up from the inside and leave me unable to go on anymore. More pathetic than I already was. I felt my mother in my fingers and I blinked to keep her out. I thought of Natalie and her eyes and her boyfriend and her father. The mental rituals I usually used weren't available to me. I was so afraid that I would have to face everything. I stopped every few stairs to catch my breath. Why didn't they make a goddamned elevator for this piece of shit building? I had thoughts of burning it down. I put those thoughts on a shit pile in the back of my head and tried to convince myself I wasn't the type of person who would ever do that.

The thing was coming for me again. My body was shaking. It was coming out my eyes and my skin was dripping off of me. I wanted my sister, I needed my sister, my mom, my dad. I needed someone.

My sister had no fucking clue what kind of shit could happen to a person in this life. She thought I could just stop drinking, just come to her house and let her nurse me back to health but what the fuck would I do with myself then? It wasn't the drinking that was the problem, but the shit beneath it. I couldn't stand the shit beneath it. I screamed for Natalie and nothing happened. I had visions of her dead on the floor and I felt like I had killed her. I remembered I was in a stairwell and kept going up to my apartment. I didn't want to have to sell my dad's guitar but the thing wasn't going to let me not. I had no other option, no other way to get what I needed. I had to take care of myself, had to believe that he would have wanted that for me.

EVICTION NOTICE. Rory Langford. Expected to evacuate. Ten days upon receiving the notice. Blah blah blah. "Fuck you." I ripped the stupid thing off my door. I wanted to piss all over the hallway. I started screaming "Fuck you, fuck you, fuck you. You want me out? Fine then. Fuck you all." I flung my door open, beat it against the wall a few times, left it hanging wide and started to throw my things into bags. All I really owned was a few books. Some shitty furniture I didn't want. These fucking pricks thought they could take my home from me, fine then fuck them. I didn't want to live here anyway in this stupid wasteland. I threw my stuff into what boxes I still had from when I moved in. I don't even deserve to exist. Natalie said so herself, she said I was just as bad as Max.

I yelled fuck you at my couch and shoved it as hard as I could against the wall, yelling and banging and making as much noise as possible. These people thought they could cheat me out of a place to live, they didn't even care what happened to me. It was becoming apparent that no one cared what happened to me.

I scoured my cupboards for alcohol. Something to drink. Something to make my heart stop beating in my eyes. I opened my screen door and threw a bag of garbage off my balcony. I walked to my kitchen, found a bottle of vodka in the cupboard above my fridge. There was a pissy little amount left in the bottom. The lid was gone, there was dust floating inside but I couldn't stop myself from putting it to my lips. I don't know how I withstood the burning in my throat and the black outer edges of the world around me. The pain made my stomach drop. Everything started to feel hazy. I felt sick, a burning, pulsing feeling in my stomach.

The blood rushed to my head and I could feel my brain rattling around in there trying to escape. Just a few more shots, just a few more shots. It will all be over if I drink just a few more shots. There was nothing left. I was on the floor, my stomach burning up through my esophagus. I could feel acid building up on my tongue. My eyes were burning. My asshole was aching.

The burning didn't stop, it wouldn't stop but I kept going. Got up to get the rest of me out of this apartment. Ignored the incessant gnawing of my gut. I threw books off my balcony, I packed my father's guitar back into its case, carried it and the one box of shit I cared about out to my car, heaving with the pain in my sides. My head was beating the shit out of itself. I couldn't feel the rest of my body, just my stomach and my throat and my head. I threw his guitar and the other shit in my trunk and went back upstairs to make sure I hadn't secretly owned something I would miss. There were books and clothes all over the floor. I couldn't see myself needing any of this. I couldn't focus long enough to decide if I did or not. I hated everyone around me, and I resented every single material possession that lingered in my line of sight. I wanted to light everything on fire. Stupid cunt landlord. I didn't even let myself see past my anger long enough to consider that I had no place to go. I didn't give a shit. So long as these assholes would never forget the pain that they caused me.

I got out my toolbox and started smashing the walls with a wrench, crying and moaning because I didn't like what I was doing, or the way my body responded with jolts of pain. Before I knew it I was unscrewing the toilet from the floor, sweat pouring all over the tiles. I leaned over once to throw up what little liquid was still left in my gut. I looked down and saw blood in my vomit. The way it merged with the pathetic empty contents of my stomach made me miss my mom. I lifted the toilet from the ground, sloshing dirty water all over my body, covering myself in blood and vomit, gritting my teeth against the weight. I put it down when I reached the open balcony door, took a long breath to try and gain my strength back. I knew it wouldn't come back so I submitted to it sucking and carried on to the edge of the balcony. I lifted the toilet as far above my head as I could, pouring the contents of the tank all over me, spotting Andy in the parking lot.

I screamed "You shady son of a bitch," and yelled loud incomprehensible grunts as I heaved the toilet off my balcony in the direction of his stupid little body. Porcelain flew everywhere, he dodged it and looked up, horrified. I could feel myself screaming, tearing apart my lungs, I could feel the flesh inside of me ripping, keeled over on the floor of my balcony, clinging to the dirty old rug on the ground. Blood came pouring out of my mouth, it hurt and tasted horrible. It clotted on the ground in front of me. I tried to stand up, the burning now in my eyes and swelling my tongue. I swallowed and tasted blood. I needed something to wash the hurt away. I yelled. It wasn't over yet. My life dragged on, no one was betting for me to win.

The people who raised me, they never expected me to succeed, they all expected me to fail but some of them just hoped they were wrong. I didn't want any more conversations with my mother about how much it hurt her just to look at me, or any more conversations with my sister where she tried to convince me that the way my mom was toward me was some sort of love that I should accept. I didn't want to think about Natalie anymore and the way her eyes glazed over at the sight of a fist, like they knew what to do, like it wasn't the first time. I didn't want to think about how I was just as bad as Max. Just as bad as Max, and the man who created me. I was a monster. I surrendered to the pain, knowing I was dying, knowing I wouldn't be lucky enough to see the light, but just as anxious to catch up to meet the darkness.

The slow ripping, blood pooling screaming of my insides pushed all my repressed thoughts back into my head. I couldn't stop the images from playing. I yelled and yelled to make it stop. I didn't want to think about my dad anymore or imagine him hanging from a shower rod. I didn't want to think anymore at all. Not about Chuck, not about

Angela. Not about the monster who caused my existence, or how I hung around the world like a damn disease. A contusion on the universe that must be stopped. I hurt the people around me just by existing and then I tried to quiet that existence, rot away slowly by myself and somehow I hurt them more.

I could feel my body floating low, low, low. I could hear a crash and a scream and a ringing in my ears that sounded like an amalgamation of everyone who ever told me they loved me. I screamed back at them to shut up. I screamed at my dad for leaving me. I screamed at the air for the way it smelled and burned my nostrils. I felt my limp body crawling across my floor, I heard a lamp shatter next to me. I kept yelling trying to silence the thing in my head. How long was this going to take? And what was happening to me? I wanted help, I wanted someone to make it stop. I wanted my dad.

My father was the one person who ever tried to help me make peace with my existence. He was the only person I ever trusted with the weight of it. Sometimes we would talk about what happened to my mom but I blocked all those conversations out until this moment. I couldn't remember a damn one until now when all I had was the burning in my lungs and the blackness behind my eyes and they started playing out in front of me like a cursed movie. I banged my head on the floor trying to get them to stop, hoping to knock myself out and just never wake up again.

I could hear myself screaming shut up over and over again as my dad flickered around the room. My dad tried so hard to love me and I didn't fucking deserve it. I didn't deserve what he did for me, or for him choosing to keep me. I didn't deserve any bite of food he put on the table for me. His face in my memory kept molding with my own and I imagined the man who intruded on my mom and I wanted to kill him. I wanted to kill the him that lived in me so that no part of him could touch my mom anymore. If I couldn't stop myself from existing the first time, I could stop myself now, and I could prevent her from any more hurt. I was finally meeting myself at a standstill. Seeing for the first time what fate had brought to me.

I got up, my shaking hands grasping the coffee table, fell down feeling my face crack. Hot liquid on my forehead or my ears or somewhere. My eyes were shaking, earthquake. I fell to the floor, misaligned kneecap. Rory screamed, he screamed loud and I apologised to him, "I'm sorry you were wasted. I'm sorry about the scraps that made you up. I'm sorry."

I was willing myself to die. If I removed myself from the earth, then mom could finally heal, she could finally let go of every part of that fucking bastard. The ground was shaking and melting and my throat was burning, bleeding. I felt my dad's

hands on me lifting me off the screaming loud floor
before everything went–

Chapter Thirty

"Dad, I know. I know what happened to mom."

The first time I saw my dad after I got out of the hospital, I made him meet me in a public park. I didn't want to give him the chance to drag me back home, I didn't want to go back there and face my mom. How could I really put the woman I loved most in the world through the torment that I acted out on myself all the time? You think when you're self-destructing that it stays within those parameters but it never does. The people around you can feel it, whether they love you or not.

"We don't have to talk about that."

I could tell it made him uncomfortable but, "I need to talk about it dad. I can hardly look at myself in a mirror because I'm so afraid I look like him."

"You don't Rory. That's one of the few things

in this world that make me have faith in anything. You are a spitting image of your mother."

"I don't think she can see that."

"She just needs time." We both stared in the same direction across the park. I was nineteen. How much time did she need? I had already waited almost two decades for her to look at me the way I looked at her, the way I needed her to.

"How long have you known?"

"What?"

"How long have you known about what happened to your mom?"

"I overheard you guys talking when I was ten."

Everything went silent, the whole park stopped murmuring, a loud kind of silence that choked me. I felt myself shift inside my body. Wondering if my dad could stand to look at me ever again now that I brought this up. If he could stomach me knowing what I was. I felt spoiled for having a life to live, for being allowed to breathe. My body didn't quite fit me but I felt like a lucky person to have it. I imagined myself sometimes in utero, floating around the substance in my mom that kept me alive and I wonder what I thought about then. If I was happy to be there. If I could feel the pressure I built in her body. I wonder if wounds have empathy for the pain they cause.

"Rory, you have to listen to me for a second. Please look at me."

I couldn't. But I pried my eyes off of the ground.

My heart was beating in my throat and I made a silent pact with myself not to open my mouth. I knew if I did, I would puke the bloody thing up or start crying. I was embarrassed to show how much this affected me, how much it hurt me. I wanted to pretend I was detached from the circumstance but I was more attached to it than I could ever help.

"You are not that man. You are a good person. Look at me."

I could feel my eyes betraying me, I just nodded. Wishing my dad wouldn't force me to look at him now while we talked about this. I wanted to run from the conversation I started. I wasn't ready to have it like I thought I had been.

"You are a good man, and you're becoming a better man every day. Your mom does love you. She just needs time to figure out how to show it." He had no idea the state my life was in. How much I drank to keep myself silent. How much I tried to kill myself without actually having the courage to kill myself.

"How much time?"

"I don't know. There isn't a blueprint for these things." He shifted and looked away.

"She's never going to love me. Just admit that, dad. You know it's true. She shouldn't have kept me."

"Don't say that, Rory. I can't speak for your mom but I have never regretted her choice to keep you. I love you and every day I see you becoming a better person and I'm proud to know you. You are my son whether you are blood or not and I will protect you for your whole life. You're funny, you're charismatic, you're gentle and loving and kind. You are not where you came from."

I was crying then and I don't remember the exact moment of collision when my dad's arm was around me but I was so aware of his body touching my body that I wanted to peel my skin off skull first and leave it laying in the park, watch my organs fall out and just cease to be.

"I love you. Please listen to me. What happened to your mom is not and never will be your fault. You are a person separate from that situation. You are a victim of your circumstance but you are not your circumstance. "

At least twice a week I would dream of attacking my own mother. I would be walking down a street and she was there, and I would be attacking her, devouring her. My own mother. The woman who gave birth to me. Some days I would wake up screaming and others I'd wake up in a cold sweat. I couldn't ever tell anybody about the dreams. I was so afraid of hurting my mom I would avoid looking her in the eye. I didn't want her to accidentally see what my mind created against my will.

I had to drink every night because it was the only thing that made the dreams stop. I snuck alcohol out of my backpack when I knew Jordan was asleep. I promised him I'd stopped, but if I went to bed a little bit tipsy, somehow I didn't dream at all and then I could have just a few minutes of peace before I had to wake up to myself again. At least this way I could rest, and I could work on being a better person during the day.

My girlfriend couldn't know, I didn't want to scare her. I wanted to tell her everything, why I couldn't touch her. She was worried that I thought she was unattractive. The intrusive thoughts stopped me. We would get so close and then I'd have to stop because I couldn't breathe, because my hands didn't feel like my own. She was growing tired of me and I could feel it. I didn't touch my own body either, I hated the idea of having a sexuality, sexual needs. I hated the idea that I could desire sex at all. It disgusted me. I wanted so much to love my girlfriend the way she deserved. She really was the greatest thing that ever happened to me at that time. I did love her, but every time she tried to touch me, I couldn't see her anymore, just flashing memories that lasted just long enough to terrorise me but not long enough for me to know what I was remembering.

She eventually broke up with me for someone who would touch her, for someone who could crawl into a bed with her without crying, for someone who could control their thoughts without drowning them. Someone who laughed more than they swore and wasn't beginning to rely on alcohol to get even the most mundane tasks done.

Dad didn't know these things. He seemed to think I was going through average and typical young adult type stuff. My body and my head felt like two different entities. No parts of me really felt attached to the others. I guess I wanted us to fix this but this was as good as it'd ever get.

We sat in the park for an hour watching the geese feed by the river. He had his arm around me the whole time and I didn't recoil under the weight of it. I melted into him, imagining my biological makeup being transplanted. I wished I could replace the parts of me that were ugly, wrong and terrible with all the parts of my father that were noble, nurturing and loyal. In that moment it felt like I could. In that moment I had hope that things could be okay and that I wasn't just an infestation of my mother's soul.

Chapter Thirty-One

That damn beeping again, it never fucking stops. I must've been in hell because I woke up to Andy standing over me.

"Oh good, you're awake. We called your emergency contact, he should be here shortly." A nurse spoke gently, brushing my shoulder as she walked past my bed. She had been adjusting the thing that was beeping, leaving the room without waiting for me to respond to her. I guess my heart rate was annoying someone besides me.

I tried to hoist my sad body up but could hardly move to look around and see where I was.

"Don't move man, you just had surgery."

"Surgery?" My voice sounded cracked and expired.

"Yeah, they sewed your stomach ulcer shut." Andy was standing over me like he actually gave a shit. It made me feel sick.

"My what?"

"You had an ulcer dumbass, it popped or whatever when you threw your toilet over your balcony. Why the fuck did you do that anyway?"

"Why are you here?"

"You threw a fucking toilet at me, then you kneeled down like you were dying. At first I thought 'fuck that guy.' But then I could hear you screaming through the ceiling of my living room. You left your door open and there you were in the middle of your floor, blood pouring out of your mouth. I've never seen anything like it." He was talking like he was describing a scene from a movie instead of a scene from my life. I hated that I had to rely on him to fill me in.

"So why am I in the hospital?" All the words he'd said to me dripped off my unreceptive mind.

"You had an ulcer and it burst. I just told you that."

"What does that mean?"

There were no nurses around to ask. Why did all of them have to be busy, leaving me with no option but to talk to Andy?

"It means that there was a hole in your stomach or something and a bunch of blood and bile and shit started leaking into your body. You threw up a lot of blood. Anyway, they gave you some stitches in your stomach."

"Cool. So can you leave now?"

"I saved your life, you know."

"What if I didn't want my life saved?"

"Why wouldn't you?"

"Not everyone wants to be on this dumb earth. It's not a preppy frat party for everyone."

"Fuck you, dude. I saved your life, you owe me one."

"Nah I don't owe you shit. Look at you, you're a fucking poser."

He smiled at me. "You're a fucking asshole."

Somehow after that we were shaking hands, bonding over the shared experience of my near death. Maybe he was an annoying shit but he had been there after all, stayed with me in the hospital a while, and when he had to leave he wished me well and said we'd go for beers sometime, and I didn't get sick at the thought of that.

"Did I hear you talking about drinking?" A condescending young male doctor came into the room just as Andy had left.

"Maybe."

"I'm afraid you'll have to cancel those plans."

"Excuse me?"

"I don't know if anyone explained to you that you had a perforated ulcer, your GI tract was–"

"Yeah, yeah I know whatever I don't care. What do you mean no drinking? Can we go back to that part?"

He squinted at me, like he was trying to figure out what I was. "Would you say you drink a lot Mr. Langford?"

"Why is that your business?"

"I'm your doctor. I performed the surgical procedure and I'll be overseeing your recovery. I need to identify the cause of the ulcer so we can prevent any further irritation. It's common for people who drink heavily to develop ulcers like these. I heard from your friend that you were doing some heavy lifting as well, which could explain the tearing of the stomach wall. Do you have a support network?"

"No. So why can't I drink?"

"I can give you some information on alcoholic recovery groups. Get you set up with an addiction counsellor."

"Oh, no I'm not an alcoholic. I just enjoy one every once in a while."

He looked at me suspiciously. "Okay, so the thing with ulcers is that any kind of irritant after an incident like this can cause a tearing of the stitches, and could cause the development of one or more ulcers. This could result in you having to get all or part of your stomach removed. I think it'd be best for you to refrain from drinking for two to six weeks at the very least."

"You're fucking kidding me. What happens if I drink?"

"At this point, you'll be out of the hospital in a few days and the stitches will be mostly healed but you could cause your stomach to haemorrhage. This could result in severe amounts of blood loss, damage to your vital organs, and, to be frank, it could be fatal.”

“Fuck.”

“I will give you a list of all the foods you should avoid, and what foods you should eat more of. It’s important that you follow the recovery guidelines to prevent further damage.”

I looked away from him. He was nosy and presumptuous and insulting and I wanted nothing to do with him. Refrain from drinking for two to six weeks, my ass. I didn’t even have a home to go to. My mother hated me, my dad was dead, I had not a friend in the world and the last time I saw my sister I’m pretty sure I burned the bridge with her as well. The doctor started to leave the room when I remembered. “Wait, someone said they were calling my emergency contact but I don’t have one.”

“You did have one on file, and the nurses contacted someone. They said they were on their way.”

“Who? If it was my dad, he died.”

“I’m not sure who it was, but whoever was on file said they were on their way.” He repeated. “They agreed to sign off on your release and keep an eye on you while you recover.”

“Who was it though?”

“I’m sorry, I don’t have the name on me right now, but they’ll be here soon I’m sure.”

“Whatever.” He was acting as though it was

none of my business whose care I was being placed in. Who the fuck would have been my emergency contact? The last time I was in the hospital the nurses were arguing with me about calling my dad. It had to be him, but how could he sign off on my release? I was afraid of who it might be. All I could do was wait and try to keep my heartbeat steady so as not to distress any nurses, or have them distress my solitude. The incision site on my stomach hurt and made it nearly impossible to sit up.

Before anyone could come back to check on me, I saw eternity fold up and pass through the curtain dividing my bed from the rest of the hospital. Jordan grinned at me. No time seemed to have passed. The hot, embarrassing cider began creeping out of the corners of those damned time capsules in my face. He put his hand on my shoulder, he always could be serious when he needed to be.

"Hey man, heard your body finally had enough of your shit."

He sat down next to me. "Don't cry Ror, it's alright."

"What are you doing here?" I was in the exact same place Jordan had come to get me the last time. Maybe the things that had happened in between now and the last time I saw him were all made up in my mind. The only thing that seemed to matter was that he was there to get me.

"The hospital called me."

I could just nod.

"Well, we're gonna have to clean this shit up aren't we?" He motioned across my body, disgusting, greasy and unshowered.

"Jordan, I'm sorry." Finally I could say to him what I always wanted to say. "I'm sorry I left."

"Yeah, I know that you dumb wanker. You're the most sorry son of a bitch I know. You don't have to apologise to me now though, you've had enough shit dumped on you that you don't need to add years-old guilt to the mix." We sat in silence for a few minutes, unsure how to break the space between the years we had lost.

"My stomach tore open because I threw my toilet off my balcony."

"So I guess you really have had a lot of shit dumped on you." We lost ourselves in laughter, all my youth coming back to me from what joy my sewn-up stomach would let me express. It hurt my guts to laugh, most of it streamed out of my eyes. I knew in that moment that I was being given something more ethereal than any other thing in the world.

"I'm not going to drink anymore Jordan."

"Jesus Christ I'm glad to hear that."

I had to stay in the hospital for two days. The nurses monitored my heart rate, my vitals, my electrolyte levels. They came to check on me once an hour at one point because my heart rate kept unexpectedly going up and then dropping really fast. Jordan stayed through the whole thing. He slept on the floor. The doctors didn't like that very much but they couldn't really stop him. You can't stop Jordan from doing something when he cares about it enough.

I stayed up all night both nights, I couldn't help it. There were strange things going on in the hall outside of my tiny curtained room. I could hear the wind leaking in through the cracks in the walls of the building. I could tell my skin was blue by the way it felt. Nurses checked on me and I muttered maybe three words to them. My stomach felt too unlike mine to talk, I thought it would try to escape me. Something in me was trying to get out, clawing its way through the membranes in my head. I couldn't see straight, room was blurry, skin was too cold, too hot, too thick.

"How are you feeling, Mr. Langford?"

"Fine."

They didn't check on me much past that, they had too many more patients to worry about and I couldn't trust them with the truth anyways. The second night was the worst. The sweat was pouring through the sheets, felt like I'd pissed myself but when I reached down to feel below my ass everything was dry. My hands felt shaky when I tried to lift them, like they had the flu. My feet were sick, nauseous. I got up once to use the bathroom. Tried not to wake Jordan. Lucky for me that he can sleep the way he can. I couldn't trust him either, who knew who he was reporting to. Some authority that could take things from me, steal from my body, steal from my mind, brainwash.

The bathroom was weird. All the walls had spots on them, the spots moved when I blinked. How could you focus on not being sick in such a dizzy place? Head was swollen on my neck. Was it always so big? Skin looked weird, puffy, lips were dry. I put water in my mouth, spat it back out. My tongue was a thick white thing jammed in my throat unprofessionally. Had they taken it out? It felt like it was glued to the back of my throat.

There was no way to know what they actually did to me. What they put in my stomach when I lay helpless on their surgical table. They put this in me, this weird crawling feeling, they dropped it in there and now I would itch forever. I scratched my stomach, the stitches. I looked at them, they kept melting and pulsing. The thing was alive.

I threw up in the toilet and it was the worst feeling I'd ever had, so bad I tried to swallow the puke back down because I felt like my body was seeking revenge on me for expelling waste. I couldn't shit. My asshole was glued shut too. There was so much glue in my body, so much weird sticky tight skin. Cotton balls in my ears. I think someone knocked on the door at one point, realised I was still in the bathroom. Suspicious, they would be suspicious. I opened it, another patient, he grunted. We were all delirious. I had to get out of this hospital.

If I tried to escape they would lock me down, one of those chairs with the straps. Keep me there till I lost my fucking mind, I know how it is, I've seen it. Can't escape, have to wait, have to lie. God, the burning in my gut, the pounding, glass breaking feeling of my temples. Everything is sucking on everything else and I can't form a clear image of the world around me. I knock into a table on my way back to my room. Makes a crash, I think. The sound is too low and far away for me to tell.

"Mr. Langford, are you okay?"

"Mhmm, tired."

I think they buy it. Do they have to buy it? Or are they pleased with themselves that I'm exactly as incapable of formulating a need for help as they wanted me to be? Body is shaking so bad. This is the end for me. I have to pretend it's okay. I can't trust the people around me, my ears are in my throat, I'm chewing on my own tongue. Where is the rest of me? They took something from me. They took me, what kind of morbid experiment was this?

"What hospital am I at?" I looked up, was talking to a wall. Thank god. If they knew I didn't know where I was, I wouldn't be able to escape. I have to just close my eyes. Have to just try to pretend...

**

Morning came in a weird blanket. I gasped when I opened my eyes, could feel myself trying to scream. Jordan was standing over me, concerned, holding a cup of water. How could I trust it was water? My throat was too dry to care, couldn't hardly swallow. I smiled at him, took a sip, watched his reaction to see if he was a normal level of pleased that I had drank the water, or a suspicious level of pleased.

"Morning sunshine, you look like the rotten end of a cow."

"Wow, thanks." My voice sounded natural. Good. If I could keep just a few words coming out, no one would know how terrified I felt on the inside.

"How are you feeling today?"

"Good. Great. I feel good."

"You ready to go home? They said they'll discharge you in about an hour or so. I figure we can head back to my place right away, get you set up. I think we should go pick up your car from your place. Not sure how much damage has been done to the apartment but we should try to clean some of that up. Don't want you going to jail after all this shit for some dumb vandalism charge. We can work something out with the landlord though, just let me do the talking."

"Okay."

"You sure you're feeling alright?"

"Yeah."

Maybe it would be hard for him to tell if I was lying or not, after all he hadn't known me for years. That's almost like not knowing me at all.

Jordan told me what he'd been up to in his life to pass the time. "I met a girl finally, but we had to break up. She was moving to Quebec for school and Lord knows I wouldn't follow anyone to Quebec for anything. Never thought I'd date again though, after what happened to Maddy."

Maddy had been Jordan's girlfriend through high school; they dated for four years. Some wild stuff had come out about her past that she couldn't properly digest. It started to really wreak havoc on her life. She was the most paranoid person any of us knew. Thought people were following her all the time, couldn't touch her own skin, that kind of thing. It got to be too much and she took her life down in one courageous go. Jordan was never the same after that.

"Maddy was really something though, wasn't she Rory? You remember she used to make us listen to those god-awful mixtapes?"

"Yeah, for hours." Our laughter was sad.

"This girl, Brianna, she was really great. Kind of reminded me of Maddy. I think you would've liked her."

"Mmm." Jordan was content talking to himself at my face so I let him go on. It distracted me from the weird tickle in my legs, the clamping of my asshole, the spasming of my stomach.

"You know Rory, I think we should get you into something you enjoy. Keep you off the drinking. When we get back to my place we should watch ballet tutorials on YouTube."

The nurse walked in, interrupting our fun. "Okay Rory, are you ready to go home?"

"Yeah."

"Okay, there's just a few basic things we need to go over first. Are you okay with your friend staying while we go over them?"

"I'm not going anywhere," Jordan said.

"Alright then. So Mr. Langford, you'll have to refrain from hard foods for about a week or two. You should be able to gauge it if you listen to your body. No crunchy stuff like chips or popcorn, try to stay away from spicy foods as well until you come back in and we get another chance to look at your stomach. Refrain from any alcohol consumption–"

Alcohol. Consumption. The thing was racing in my chest, tingling around in there trying to get out.

"Try not to smoke, or cut down at least. We want to limit the possibility of any infection or further perforation. I have a pamphlet of foods you should add to your diet, and foods you should avoid. Here, I'll leave it with you and if there are any complications– any pain, or diarrhoea, headaches, insomnia, vomiting– please come back to see us immediately. I'll check your vitals one last time, and then you can be on your way. Do you have any questions?"

"No."

"I have a question." Jordan. "What happens if he drinks?"

"If he drinks it could cause the ulcer to perforate again. We have to let the stitches dissolve and the wound on his stomach heal. He has limited stomach acid right now and scarring on the GI tract, any amount of irritation can cause a haemorrhage or more serious complications. We can't know for sure what might happen. Everyone responds differently but it would be wise if alcohol was avoided all together. We can't take any chances."

Jordan looked at me. "You got that?"

"Yeah. Got it."

The nurse checked my vitals which were all suspiciously normal considering how shaky and out of whack I felt. My body was shrinking and expanding, my fingers were twitching, my brain was screaming. I couldn't tell her any of this, I just wanted out of this fluorescent-infested freak place. Something was running around inside my arms, trying to chase my limbs from my body. I smiled and walked as steadily to Jordan's car as possible.

"You wanna stop at your place first and deal with that shit or head back to mine to rest a bit?"

"Whatever."

Jordan started heading toward his place." Before we do anything we gotta get you a shower, dude. You smell like rotting fish."

Chapter Thirty-Two

The shower was weird and sticky, I forgot to take my socks off. I peeled them off and heard them slap against the bathroom floor. I needed something to drink, my fingers won't bend properly without lubrication. I itched and abstained, and I clawed my skin, the unscratchable itch. I wanted to yell out loud in the shower, I hoped for falling, cracking my head. I just wanted to be unconscious for a while. I could feel the water moving through my body, I felt thin, like a moth-eaten bedsheet. I tried to touch my own skin, there was plastic wrap over the incision site. Was I supposed to be showering? Maybe I couldn't breathe because of the plastic holding my stomach in, maybe I needed to take it off. I itched the tape holding it on, my skin felt disgusting underneath, put the tape back on, couldn't face my body. Fuck the thing if it wanted to suffocate. I ran my fingers through my hair, pulled on my scalp, my forehead was tingling, I squished my face to move the sensation around, still couldn't feel.

"You ready to go?" Jordan walked up to me, caught me staring off at one of his weird pictures of Karl Marx.

"What? Yeah. Sure."

"You okay?" He was looking down at my dripping feet. "You need a pair of socks?"

"What? How many times a day are you gonna ask me that, yeah I'm fine, my socks are fine."

"Alright." He looked at me apprehensively. "Let's get going then."

I lost the minutes from when I was in the shower to when I was dressed on the couch, to when I was in the car, time was halting. Stopping and starting over. I felt like I was walking through a never ending time loop. I wanted to ask Jordan where we were. Nothing looked familiar. My face scared me the most when I caught sight of it. Who the fuck was that guy? I had stitches in my forehead, long dark circles carrying down to my cheeks. I didn't recognise myself, couldn't look at myself. My skin looked yellow, my breath tasted like hell.

We got to my building, I wondered about Andy. I started remembering that day. The ripping, the shattering white porcelain on the pavement, the screams that came from some part of me I didn't want to know about. The moaning, blood between my teeth.

"I can't go in there." This time my voice didn't mask any of the panic I felt inside.

"You can't just leave it like that man. We have to get in there. But, we can take a minute if you want."

"The cops are in there."

He really looked concerned now. "No, they aren't Rory. And if they are I'll deal with them. Just worry about making steps to fix shit. Are you sure you're okay?"

"Yes," I yelled at him. "Fuck, sorry."

"Okay, should we go back to the hospital?"

"No, let's just go. Let's just get it over with."

I focused all my energy on cleaning the apartment, picking drywall off the ground, throwing clothes in garbage bags, ignoring how the room shifted in and out of place every time I bent my body. Jordan made a comment about how I'd really gone all Rory on the place. I told him not to make me into a verb. He laughed. I didn't. He spent most of the time talking about the problems of the world, making light where he could, coming up with revolutionary ideas on how he could fix them. Started talking about pyramid schemes. I forgot how this dude could ramble.

I couldn't focus on a word he was saying, my skin was way too hot, it was incinerating every thought that popped up. "God damnit." I accidentally said out loud.

"What's up?"

"Nothing. I stepped on something sharp."

Jordan looked at the floor, nothing was there. I knew he was about to ask me if I was okay again so I went to the bathroom, closed the door. The walls were vibrating, everything was really fucking me around. I could feel myself swaying. I sat quietly on the floor, feeling my forehead, it was drenched. My hair was maybe still wet from the shower. Shower. I needed a shower. Had I showered? I turned on the tap, locked the door, sat in the tub with all my clothes on. They stuck to my body, started to cool it down, I layed down to relax. The water kept leaving the tub. Forgot to put the drain stopper in, couldn't reach it, shoved my heel in the drain to stop the water from abandoning me. Could feel a sharp pain moving up my ankle. Jordan started knocking on the door, getting more and more frantic but the world was finding its peace with me in that little porcelain tub. I laughed at the hole in the floor where the toilet should be. Stupid fuckers got what was coming to them. There was a spider running across the floor towards me, it stopped, ran back and crawled into a hole in the wall, even it was afraid of me. "Fuck off then, weird little ant." I laughed at it.

"Rory, open the door. What the fuck are you doing?"

"I gotta shower man, I'll help you clean in a minute, I just feel really gross." The dried puke from my shirt was peeling off and floating in the water, I tried to scoop it up, get it out, it separated in weird floating chunks. The water was turning blue and green and clear. "I think the bathroom's flooding." I called out to Jordan. I tried to reach for the tap but it kept getting further away from me. My skin was so hot, so hot my eyes kept closing, my breath kept stopping. "It's too hot in here." I touched the outside of the bathtub, I felt it move, it was weird and rubbery. "Why does it feel like that?"

"Why does what feel like what?" Jordan was banging on the door hard. "Rory, open the door now or I'll break it down."

"Don't do that. I need my damage deposit." I laughed.

"You think you're getting your damage deposit back? You threw your toilet off your balcony you dumbass. Open the fucking door Rory."

"I can't Jordan. It's too hot."

I could hear him slamming his body against the door. I could feel the force of the water trying to suck me down the drain. I had to go wherever the things wanted me to go. Skin was shrinking, tight, pruning to my body. "No, fuck off." I yelled. I wasn't ready to go down, get out, have it out with my world, life, safe. I was not safe. I wrenched my heel from the drain, outlined the circular indent with my fingertips, looked down. There were things coming out of the drain, there were hands wrapping around my toes. I kicked at them, I splashed water into my face, the tub was draining, the world was opening, I needed to find a way out. Water was filling my head, could hear it drowning me, could feel myself sinking. Crawled out of tub. Tub had eyes. Skin, where is my skin, I can feel skeleton, poking out, eyebrows are coming unstitched. Banging on the door, "Who's there?" a man yelled back. "Open the fucking door Rory." Could hear him panting.

"What do you need? I'm just gonna be busy, out in a while, I'll see you in a minute." Vomit came out with the words, it spelled my father's name on the floor, it shone in my eyes. It laughed, it blinded me. Eyes were turning black, couldn't see everything at once. I reached to turn off the light, I fell down on the floor, vomit covering my cheeks. Hilarious. So hot, touched forehead to floor, felt it quake, the earth is shaking it's fucked, it's coming up to get me. "Dad, I never got to ask you why you never went to Indonesia." The world came with its borders. There was grass coming through the floor, it was winter, snowing, what year was it. I'm sixteen, nineteen, where am I? Banging, splintering wood. "Leave me alone dad, I don't want to talk about it." Someone screamed my name. I called out for air. Where's oxygen? Nitrogen in head, there's an ulcer on my eye, the world is gone, losing itself in sections. Losing itself, losing itself, losing itself, losing itself, losing itself, I want off. Out. "Let me out." My fist is pulling apart, I can see it hitting the floor, the floor blinks, it responds. I kiss my own arm, sweat, water, salt. "Dad, I need to come home please let me come home." I miss him so much I can't let it go, can't let it go, can't let it go, let it go, let it go, let it go let it go let it go letigoletigo letititititititititititittttttttt.........

"He's not responsive yet. Had a major seizure. He's stable, should be awake soon. We've got him hooked up to an IV."

Soft voices, hollow as angels and quietly dusting off the blur of my mind.

"Why did he have a seizure?" This kind of angel weeps. "Is he going to be okay?"

"Yes, ma'am he's going to be just fine. He was having severe alcohol withdrawal, but he's going to be just fine. We'll keep him stabilised here as long as needed."

"Oh god." The weeping. The long, long gasps. Who told her to weep like that? Who teaches us to weep like that?

I could feel my eyes peeling open, slowly, dry lids peeling back like dead fish off the pavement. Mom looked right into me, caught the place where the ache hurt most. Collapsed onto me. I felt my arms wrap around her, my shoulders wet with her rejoice.

"Rory! Oh god, my sweet, sweet baby boy. Oh thank God. Thank God Rory," She kissed me, stroked my hair, shook, held me. I felt wet leak out of my face. I kissed her forehead, she said, "I'm so glad you're okay, Rory. My sweet, sweet boy. I'm so glad you're alive."

Acknowledgments

Many addicts, myself included, inspired the stories and the harrowing emotive experiences in these pages. I will not name anyone directly, but I thank them in my heart for sharing their solidarity, their space and their love with me. This book is for anyone whose rock bottom beat them back and who had to crawl out of it without a loving support network. Often, we the addicted, the Mad and the ill have to look out for one another, and so I give my infinite thanks to every person who shared cigarettes or conversation with me at the hospital, every nurse or patient who offered me an extra blanket on a cold night, or who talked me out of a dark place. Thank you to every person who fed me, held space for me and made me laugh. Thank you to Farrah for putting lavender on my pillow and giving me rides to the airport, for buying me chocolate croissants and giving me extra butter for my toast. Thank you to Penny for the danishes, the laughs, and the extra strong coffee.

Thank you to the spaces that I occupied while writing this book: The University of

Alberta Hospital, The Rutherford Library, John L. Haar Library, the Edmonton International Airport, various parkades and train stations and the backs of classrooms (oops).

Thank you to Harman Burns for believing in this book so much, for lending me your basement floor to scatter the manuscript across in order to figure out what I was trying to say. Thank you for reading every draft and answering all my frantic phone calls when I was sure Rory was trying to kill me.

Thank you to Ryan for sharing your stories with me. I love you very much.

Thank you to every philosophy professor I've ever had. I promise you inspired none of the characters in this book.

Thank you to Miette and Whisky Tit Books for giving Rory such a perfect home and for loving him as much as I do.

Additional thanks, in no particular order, to my old friends Bryer, Kristina and Jacob; to Cliff and Sherron Burns, Nick Mitchell, Hamdi Isaawi, Dr. Susan Mills, Dr. Ruth Martin, and Deb Willis, all of whom supported early drafts of this novel in various ways.

Lastly, thank you to Deb McCandless, for your love and your wisdom. You gave me the strength to be who I am and say what I mean. I love and miss you for all time.

About the Author

Niamh Burns (they/them) is a chronically ill, non-binary, femme Irish poet and artist who writes from the unceded, ancestral territories of the Musqueam, Squamish and Tsleil-Waututh peoples. Their work has appeared in *The Anti-Languorous Project*, *The West Review*, *Visitant Literary Journal* and elsewhere. They are the author of *Frances* and *In Back of Heaven*.

About the Publisher

Whisk(e)y Tit is committed to restoring degradation and degeneracy to the literary arts. We work with authors who are unwilling to sacrifice intellectual rigor, unrelenting playfulness, and visual beauty in our literary pursuits, often leading to texts that would otherwise be abandoned in today's largely homogenized literary landscape. In a world governed by idiocy, our commitment to these principles is an act of civil service and civil disobedience alike.